Parsons Unknown

By
S.P.R.Foulger

To Diana

S.P.R. Foulger
6/8/19

Parsons Unknown

Copyright © Stuart Foulger

All characters and place names, other than those well-established such as towns and cities, are fictitious and any resemblance is purely coincidental.

All rights reserved.
The moral right of the author has been asserted.
No part of this publication may be reproduced, stored in a retrieval system, or transmitted in any form or by any means, without the prior consent of the author, nor be otherwise circulated in any form of binding or cover other than that in which it is published and without a similar condition being imposed on the subsequent purchaser.

Authors Note

This is my first book and hopefully it will bring you happiness and entertainment. Yes, I am a proud and genuine Christian, but to the best of my knowledge, there is no village called Kirby Maltings, at least in Norfolk! I have not met a Vicar called Jack Parsons although this is a vocation that requires great skill and commitment. I must record my thanks to Di Bettinson for the excellent illustration on the front. I also must thank Helen Thwaites for her help in publishing this. I also thank Catherine Quinlan for her wonderful help too. Di Bettinson has written a number of books as has Helen Thwaites both under her own name and under the name, Elizabeth Manning Ives.

S.P.R. Foulger

Chapter One

The sad but fast walking figure in the ill matched clothes did not look as if he had enjoyed a happy or rewarding life. He wondered to himself as he wandered by himself how so many things had happened so quickly. Had this all been a dream? It might be possible that he was still drunk, but no, he knew that this was not the answer. He had in the last few weeks or maybe it had just been days, experienced more adventure, more mystery and more happiness and kindness than he had encountered in his entire previous life. No, this has not been a dream, these things had really happened. The really sad part was that all this had now come to an end and he was now facing a cold reality.

It had all started on a wet and blustery night when he had called round to the house of his wife's best friend. Both ladies were out playing Bingo, so, being the considerate fellow he was, Jack Parsons had come to visit the other lonely husband with a six pack of beer. A loud knock at the door and Jack was in. The other husband, Alec Smith, was a quiet and reserved man, but he never argued with

Jack, was completely honest and more importantly, he always laughed at Jack's jokes. He was therefore quite an exceptional fellow!

Jack took off his coat in the sitting room.

"Bit cold tonight," he said.

Alec smiled and nodded. Jack would normally have drunk from the cans, but Alec was almost middle class and his wife was extremely house-proud. Alec brought in a tray with two glasses.

"Blimey, said Jack, "I'm in the First Class Carriage tonight."

Alec smiled and nodded, this was something that he did a lot of. Jack poured his beer dutifully into a glass, gave a quick "Cheers" and then downed it in a few gulps.

"So," said Jack, "How have things been with you this month?" Alec shrugged his shoulders as he often did and replied, "Well Penelope is still heavily involved with amateur dramatics and she has brought home ten suitcases all with different costumes. They take up quite a bit of room, but well, if it makes her happy..." Alec's reply vanished almost as quickly as Jack's first can of drink. Jack helped himself to a second can enquiring, "So what sort of costumes then?" eager to hear stories or gossip. Alec shrugged his shoulders and rising from the chair, he said, "I'll bring them down."

After a few minutes Alec reappeared with two suitcases. It was obvious from his breathing that they were rather heavy. "I'll get all the others as well," he said. Although Jack could be an opportunist, he was a fair man too.

"No," he said, "Two is enough, Alec, I was just curious. Don't forget to have some beer yourself boy." Alec opened the two suitcases. One contained a clown costume and a Deep Sea Divers outfit, the other contained a Cowboys outfit and a Vicars costume. Jack roared with laughter, "So Alec, my old son, does she let you play with them?" Alec shook his head.

Jack downed his second beer and opened his third can. Alec smiled and brought a bottle of Whiskey from the cabinet.

"Blimey," said Jack, "you really are pushing the boat out tonight. This is almost mutiny my old son." Alec took two glasses and gave Jack a treble dram. Not wishing to be impolite, Jack downed it quickly. He held out the glass for the customary refill. It was true that Jack did love his drink, but Alec had never seen his friend either drunk or violent. Would this evening be any different? Alec guessed not. Jack downed the second one with the same flair and ease.

"Come on," said Jack, "One more for old time's sake." Alec again obliged. Jack was an unusual character, but he had a heart of gold and he was a good and loyal friend. Jack downed it again in a gulp. Three Whiskeys and three beers later, Jack was merry but seemed to be fairly sober.

"I just don't know where you put it Jack," said Alec.

Alec got up from his chair and switched on the television with the remote control.

"I know," he said, "but there's so much clutter in here, I have to stand up to do it. I hope you don't mind, but I usually watch the news now. I keep hoping that I will see something cheerful and uplifting."

Now it was Jacks turn to shrug his shoulders, "Too many bad folk around, for there to be any good news mate," he said. The report on Global Warming cheered neither man up. Alec sighed and switched the television off. Jack took his fourth can of beer and started to examine the costumes.

"Alright," he said after a few minutes, "Who is going to be the clown?" Alec smiled and started to try on the costume.

"Well," said Alec, "You certainly can't be the Vicar as you've been drinking!"

Jack laughed, "Says who?"

After a few minutes the sober and the drunk had been replaced by a Clown and a Vicar. Alec went up to the mirror and turned around to make a witty remark but saw that Jack was now sound asleep.

A sudden thought came into Alec's mind. If his wife came home and found Jack asleep and drunk on the sofa, she would be furious. He had to try and wake his friend up and get him placed in a taxi as soon as possible. Friday nights were nearly always busy but he had to take a chance and hope for the best. Finding the number he phoned the firm and ordered the cab. He was told that it could take an hour. Although it was getting closer to his wife's arrival home, Alec took the optimistic view that this would give him time to sober his friend up. Alec went into the kitchen to make some strong and necessary coffee.

Alec loved tea and nearly always preferred it to coffee, however it was the latter that was needed now. He knew that he could not operate the expensive machine that his wife had brought, so it would have to be the instant type. The kettle with its boiling sound drowned out the knock at the front door. The man who was asleep on the sofa though did hear it. Jack walked to the front door and opened it.

"Whatcha," he said, "He has double glazing already." The cabbie smiled "No sir, this is the taxi that you ordered." Jack gave a quizzical look.

"Well," he said, "when opportunity knocks, you have to answer the door."

Jack yelled out to Alec "I'm off now, have the rest of the beer, but don't do anything daft." Jack and the cabbie got into the taxi.

"Where to?" asked the driver. "Home of course," Jack replied. The cabbie refrained from an angry response. Well the man was a vicar even if he had been drinking.

The cabbie tried again "Where to then Mr. Reverend?" Jacks mind was hazy. He said "To the River Bank." The cabbie shrugged his shoulders and set off for the unusual destination. The cabbie turned his radio up loud enough to hear the weather warning "A thunderstorm and torrential rain are set to hit the mainland in the next hour. Please do not travel unless absolutely necessary." The cabbie was amazed that anyone would want to go to the Riverbank at this time of night and with this sort of weather warning in place. However, he had collected all sorts of customers over the years and he had bills to pay and a job to do, plus the man was a vicar albeit an eccentric one and anyway they had just arrived there.

Jack got out of the cab and searched through his pockets. They felt different and he could not find any money.

"Just a minute," he said to the cabbie. He started to walk to the edge of the water and muttered to himself. "That's not right, this is not my place." All of a sudden, the rain started. The cabbie decided that he was wasting his time and thought the best thing to do was to go back to the address where he had collected the unusual passenger, after all the Vicar had called out to someone as he had left.

As the cab pulled away, the rain became much heavier and the thunder started. Jack was right near the water's edge when a bolt of lightning struck him. The impact of this caused him to topple into a rowing boat and with the extra weight of Jack, the loosely tied rope became untangled. The rain was pelting the whole town and the boats were moving around although the one that Jack was in was the only one that had become loose. The boat started to move further out along the river.

About ten minutes later a concerned Alec had paid the cabbie and explained that his friend lived at 2 The River Banks. The cabbie set off to find the man that he now knew was not a Vicar, but they were destined never to meet again. As the thunder and lightning in combination with the torrential rain fascinated some in the town, but disturbed others, the boat with the man in the Vicars costume was moving a great distance, but apart from the rocking and swaying the passenger was getting the best night's sleep that he had enjoyed for ages.

Chapter Two

As Saturday morning dawned in the Norfolk village of Kirby Maltings, nobody would have guessed that the place had been visited by a terrible thunderstorm during the previous night and the early hours of the morning. The place was unknown to several folk more than fifty miles away. However it boasted a village green, a post office, a public house and a lovely building of worship called St. Georges Church.

The early morning was often a good time for dog walkers and Barney Brown was no exception. He and his Lurcher dog, whom he called Munchkin, always walked at this time of the day. As they left the woods and made their way to the river's edge, something aroused Munchkin's curiosity. He ran ahead and stopped right next to a rowing boat. He ran back to Barney and then back to the boat barking loudly.

"What's the matter, Munchkin?" said Barney, "It's only a blinking boat." As Barney reached the boat, the sight that greeted him made him gasp. In the rowing boat was a Vicar who was sound asleep. If that was not enough, there was a faint aroma of alcohol. Munchkin's barking finally aroused the sleeping Vicar.

Jack opened his eyes. He couldn't believe it. Was this a dream? He was not in his bed, he was in a boat. What was this dark outfit that he was wearing? Also, who was this tramp with a large dog?

"Good morning, sir," said Barney. "We are about due for a new Vicar. I will be honest with you though sir, we did not expect you to arrive by boat." Jack was stunned. He could remember a few things. He recalled, Alec, the drinks, oh yes, the drinks. Then the pieces came together. He recalled the costumes the taxi cab, the river, oh and the bright light.

Jack got up and stepped out of the boat.

"I don't suppose you have a phone on you by any chance?" Barney shook his head "Me and Munchkin have no time for phones sir. However, I know for a fact that there is one at the Vicarage," He paused, "Your new home sir." The tramp and his dog departed, "I will get Dirk to fetch you, sir." Barney called out. Jack put his face in his hands. Oh my word he thought, not only have I got myself lost, these folk will think I'm their new Vicar!

After a very brief time, Jack heard the

roar of a motor bike and as it came into view he saw that it was fitted with a sidecar. The driver climbed off and walked up to Jack with his hand stretched out.

"Hello sir, I'm Dirk Connors the verger." Dirk seemed to be a pleasant and unassuming man with a pronounced Norfolk accent. Well Jack assumed it was a Norfolk one. Jack took a chance. "This is Norfolk, isn't it?" Dirk smiled, "Oh sir, I can see you have a sense of humour. The other bloke before you certainly did not have that." Jack realised that he was in a difficult situation and he did not want to make matters any worse. At least this well-built fellow seemed to be a decent sort of person. Jack figured that the best thing would be to go with this man to the Vicarage, make a telephone call, book a taxi and then leave at night time. After all he reasoned, nobody would miss him, nobody would be upset. Jack did notice though that Dirk did not confirm whether they actually were in Norfolk.

Jack climbed into the sidecar and thought to himself that at least the journey would be a smooth and steady one. He could not have been more wrong. Dirk drove at breakneck speed. Jack was able to see the scenery, but as he was holding on for dear-life, there was not much of a chance to observe and get his bearings. He saw just one road sign informing him that London was a long way away. At least the local villagers had a sense of humour. They finally reached their destination, it was a large Victorian building set in a large overgrown garden and the house was surrounded by trees. It did not look particularly inviting.

As Jack got out of the sidecar, he realised that he must have looked shocked as Dirk said to him, "Your new home, Sir. It looks better once you go inside." Jack hoped that Dirk's honesty was equal to his friendliness. They went inside as Dirk opened the front door and gestured for him to come in. The hallway was long and dark. There was a Grandfather clock, several pictures and a wide staircase. Even though it was November, Jack still found the place to be rather cold.

"So, I guess the central heating isn't on?" he asked. Dirk grinned, "No sir, we don't have anything like that. Your predecessor used to say that hard work was the best way to keep warm. Between you and me sir, he was not a very easy man to work for. He upset quite a few of the villagers. However, I am sure that it will be different with you, sir. You look to be a nice and genuine man."

Jack felt just a little bit guilty, but only for a few seconds. Well, he did not want to come here, wherever he was. He did not say that he was a vicar and anyway what could he do for the village? It was a place that he did not even known the name of. Dirk called out to him, "Why not have a look around sir and I will bring you a nice cup of tea." Jack went through one door, it was a long thin lounge but he only saw a settee and three chairs. There was no television. He went back into the hall and tried another room. This looked more promising, there was a bookcase, a desk, a chair and on the desk was a rather old fashioned telephone. He walked around the desk and opened the top drawer. He found a small magazine that read: *Kirby Maltings Newsletter.*

Jack flipped through the pages. There were articles about church events, coffee mornings and a few business adverts, one of those claimed that it was the best bakery in Norfolk. So, that was it. He was in Norfolk, and now he knew the name of the village he could plan his departure. Well, escape seemed to be a rather dramatic way of putting it! His thoughts were interrupted by Dirks rather loud cough.

"Excuse me sir, I know that you have only just arrived, but a young lady wishes to speak to you, it is rather urgent." Jack grimaced. Here he was planning to leave and now he had a visitor. Well he figured it was probably just a neighbour who wanted to say a quick hello. Jack composed himself, "Yes alright, no problem my old son."

A young nervous lady, who appeared to be in her early thirties, came into the study. She held out her hand, "Thank you so much for seeing me, I know that you have only just arrived, but I really need to talk to someone." Jack shook her hand and gestured for her to sit down on the chair that was not really his. Suddenly the lady started to cry. Jack felt in his pocket for a handkerchief, but there was nothing. What a start he thought. Fortunately the lady had her own one. Dirk came in with a tray of tea with two cups. Dirk was obviously very efficient.

The lady composed herself. "By the way, my name is April, April Jones." Jack coughed, "Just call me Jack, all my friends do." The lady smiled. Jack gestured to the tea tray. "Help yourself, sweetheart." The lady took a cup of tea but immediately her hands started shaking. Jack took the cup from her gently and gestured with a thumbs up sign. "Look," he said, "It's okay, you didn't spill the tea, so spill the beans instead." The lady gave a half smile.

Her story was a sad yet unusual one. She recounted how much she loved her husband and how they had always trusted each other, then all of a sudden he appeared to be acting strangely. He started going out nearly every evening for about three hours and until yesterday he refused to tell her where he was going. Then yesterday evening he had snapped at her and told her he was going to the pub. However, April's friend who was in the pub that very evening with her cousin, said that he definitely was not there. Jacks head was spinning, he was a Car Salesmen not an Agony Uncle.

Dirk popped his head around the half open door. "Excuse me sir, but there is a telephone call and it is most urgent." Dirks interruption was just what Jack needed, he knew that he had to have time to think about this. It was a sign of his confusion that he did not even ask who the phone call was from. Walking into the hallway, he realised that there must be another phone line, as the one on his desk had been silent. Dirk lead Jack into the kitchen and put a finger to his lips.

"I am not one to eavesdrop sir, but I can enlighten you in this matter. The lady's husband is going to Night School to be a Plumber. He wants to tell her when he has qualified. They do not have much money, sir." Jack was astounded, this bloke Dirk was obviously very handy and that was good, but equally he might possibly notice if Jack made plans to leave and also it probably would not take him too long to figure out that this man from the boat was not a proper Vicar. Jack nodded and said, "Thanks."

Jack returned to the study and walked straight up to April. "Listen sweetheart," he said, "I know you ladies have your female intuition, well us geezers have it too. I really think that there is some logical explanation for all of this." He took a guess, "Does your old man go to church by any chance?" April nodded. Jack was relieved. It was plain sailing now.

"I will have a chat with him then, bloke to bloke." April smiled. This seemed to be enough for her. She thanked him for his time and left. A few moments later, a smiling Dirk came in and collected the tea tray.

"Male intuition eh, sir?" he said.

Jack grinned, "Well, it's not a bad start, is it?"

Dirk nodded in agreement. Jack suddenly remembered that this was a Saturday afternoon and whilst he hardly ever set foot in a church, he knew that Sunday was the day for most church services. Surely though they would not expect a brand new Vicar to start preaching straight away? He walked into the kitchen, the room was huge with a table and chairs, an Aga stove and even a settee. Dirk was washing dishes. Jack had to make this casual.

"So Dirk, how long have you been the verger here?" It was an attempt to get his verger to open up. Dirk did not hesitate, "Three years sir." Jack realised that he would have to be more direct. "So, what time is the service tomorrow?" Dirk looked puzzled. It was clear that he expected Jack to know this.

"Well sir, the morning one is at ten o'clock and there is evensong at six-thirty." Jack was stunned. Good grief, he thought to himself, I hardly ever go to church and now they want two sermons from me. This was getting to be really serious, in fact bordering on the downright risky. He had to leave and quickly, but just how? He did not relish the idea of running away in the middle of the night, but equally could he order a taxi without Dirk knowing. He thought again. Could he pretend to be ill, so he did not have to give a sermon? As for April, well surely Dirk could sort that issue out. He was getting really flustered. All his life he had ducked and dived to get himself out of trouble, but this was unlike anything else that he had encountered before.

That night as the clock chimed eleven, Jack quietly and carefully tiptoed into the hallway and gently unlocked and opened the front door. He had heard Dirk climb the staircase about an hour ago, making allowances for the fact that not everyone falls asleep immediately on climbing into bed, he thought that an hour should be suffice. The idea of an escaping Vicar was an ironic thought but there again he was not a real Vicar, just the victim of mistaken identity.

Jack closed the front door behind him. Freedom! He moved quickly into the front garden. It was like a jungle, but being a tough character, an overgrown mass of plant life would not be intimidating to him. He made his way past the front gates, he had done it!

All he needed now was to find a phone box, ring for a taxi and he would be back home. In a few months' time nobody would remember him and anyway the real Vicar would probably have arrived.

He turned towards the village and just like a bolt from the blue, he saw Barney and Munchkin.

"Hello Sir, I guess you must have insomnia, I had a sister that suffered from that," Jack groaned inwardly. Barney seemed a decent bloke and Jack certainly did not mind dogs, but he really wished that he had turned right instead. Still he had to reply.

"Well, I guess I thought that I would wander around and try to get my bearings." Jack knew the explanation was weak, but surely this other man would swallow his story. Sadly it was not going to work.

"Actually sir, it's lucky for you that you ran into us. The roads here are very narrow and if you stray too far into the grassy areas, there are some marshes and well sir, if you fell into them at this time of night, then who would know?" Jack pondered that one. Maybe he had been lucky. Munchkin barked and Barney said, "Don't worry sir, that was probably a fox, my friend here sees and hears everything. I used to take him to church with me, but the previous Vicar put a stop to that."

Jack thought for a second, "Well, I don't know how long I am going to be here, but do feel free to bring him."

Barneys face lit up, "Bless you sir, you are a gentleman."

Jack made his way back to the Vicarage. He gingerly opened the front door and came face to face with Dirk.

"Hello sir, do you want some cocoa?" Jack replied with a mumbled, "Thanks." So, now he was in a right situation, tomorrow at ten, just over ten hours away now, he would have to stand up in church and preach. He pondered for a moment, he wondered if he could get some ideas from Dirk. The arrival of a large mug of cocoa on a tray gave him a chance.

Jack tried the casual approach, "Tell me Dirk, were you here when the previous Vicar had his first service? I would say that you can probably remember a lot of what he said." There was a moments silence although it seemed much longer.

"Well sir, I can't remember verbatim. I am a verger, not a curate." Jack had to think fast, Dirk had just used two unfamiliar words.

"Alright then, let's imagine, just for fun, that you were the new Vicar, well then, what would you preach about?" Dirk seemed to be genuinely puzzled.

"Oh no sir, I am not the Vicar type." Jack was finding this to be very tricky. Dirk was no country bumpkin yet Jack was finding him to be a very difficult person to extract information from. Jack wondered briefly, if maybe Dirk was just acting like an innocent, but then again he would not use words that Jack had never heard before. As if by a sudden piece of good luck, Dirk opened up.

"Well sir, if you want my take on this, then I would say that a Vicar should always use the Bible. Any Vicar who does not use that book is not worth listening to, in my opinion."

Dirk then wished Jack a quick goodnight and departed up the stairs. Jack walked into the study and took a bible from the bookcase. Jack took his coat off, picked up the good book and sat on the chair. He realised that he had never read this book before. Oh yes, he had heard of it, but the time had never been right for him, well that was his story.

Chapter Three

Jack started on the *Book of Genesis* and after reading a few pages he fell asleep. He did not often dream, but this time it was different. He saw a village church and he was inside it and right at the front. He was frightened. Folk were staring at him, he did not know what to say. Dirk appeared with the Bible in his hands, Jack started to read. The congregation looked content. Jack was calm. He woke up suddenly. He was still in the study and according to his watch it was six o'clock. Well at least he had a little time to gather his thoughts, have a shower, eat breakfast and so some more reading.

Time really did fly for Jack. The shower, the dressing and the breakfast took an incredible two and a half hours. He went back into the study and continued to read the book of Genesis. He found the story to be really emotional and also interesting. He could not help thinking about how little he knew about the Bible. Oh yes, he had heard of Adam and Eve, but that was about it. A sudden thought did occur to him. If the church folk had been going there for a long time, they would know these Bible Books very well and they would therefore be quick to notice any errors on the part of their new Vicar. That settled it. Jack was taking the Bible with him, he would not rely on his part-time memory.

At half past nine, he left the Vicarage. Dirk followed him outside and pointed to the motorbike. Well, given what Barney had said about the marshes, perhaps Dirks vehicle would be safer. Jack climbed into the sidecar and off they went. Jack did not see many folk about on the route. Maybe the congregation would be small in number he hoped. He did not know anyone who went to church back home. However, he thought that on reflection, it might be better if there were lots of people. They might be more focused on each other instead. As they reached the grounds of St. Georges Church, Jack realised that whether the congregation was big or small, he was going to have to do something that he had never done before. There were no butterflies in the church grounds but plenty of them in his stomach.

Jack got out of the sidecar and walked along the churchyard and into the tall and rather old church. The front door was already open and there were a few folk sitting at the front. The questions began and all from himself. Where did he sit? How long was the service expected to be? Were there many hymns to be sung? Did he have to choose them? He was uncomfortable with the idea of an improvised service, but realistically, he simply had no choice. He looked around having heard more footsteps. More folk had entered the church. The average age of the congregation so far, he guessed was about seventy. One of the folks at the front, an old lady with a green jacket stood up and greeted him.

"Good morning sir. We are so glad to have a new Vicar, we really need one in Kirby Maltings."

After a minutes silence, Jack remembered that he had not replied as he should have done. "That's quite alright my dear. My pleasure, indeed my honour." He thought for a second. She seemed to be a nice lady. He needed a few friendly faces in the pews. "So, what's your name sweetheart?" It was the best line that he could think of.

They lady smiled, "its Mabel, Mabel Smith." Jack shook hands. "Well it's good to meet you Mabel." He paused, he had to take a chance. "You know Mabel I want this to be a happy relationship here. So, just out of interest, how long should the services be? I don't want folk falling asleep." He smiled and was pleased that this gesture was returned. She seemed to be a very sweet lady and he had clearly made a new friend.

"Oh about an hour and a half in the morning and an hour in the evening, "she replied. He knew that it was going to be a long and dramatic day, but at least he had made one new friend. His thoughts were interrupted by a less friendly voice.

"Mabel, the Vicar is a busy man, he does not have time to gossip when he is working." Jack saw a tall well-dressed lady who seemed to be about the same age as Mabel, but nowhere near as friendly. Jack held out his hand, but the lady did not respond. She appeared to be studying him and Jack could tell from the brief few moments that he had seen her, she was a potential troublemaker. "And who would you be?" asked Jack. The reply was icy cold "Mrs. Thompson." She nodded quickly and walked past him.

Jack could see more folk entering the church. The age range did not appear to change. Some looked at him. Some were talking and glancing in his direction. He felt a tap on his shoulder, it was Dirk.

"I think that you'll need to start in a few minutes, sir." Jack nodded in response. Dirk led him up to the pulpit. There was a hymn book there. Jack noticed that there was nobody at the church organ. Dirk seemed to read his mind on this one.

"I am afraid that the regular organist has the flu, sir... I don't suppose you can play?" Jack was not amused but the last thing he wanted to do was create enemies therefore he let the remark go unanswered. A few more folk drifted in. A middle aged couple and a nervous looking young lady who appeared to be in her early twenties. Dirk coughed and showed Jack the watch on his wrist. It was now ten o'clock. The time had arrived.

Jack cleared his throat. "Right, good morning everybody. Lovely day for it."

Mrs. Thompson looked startled. He had to remember though, that she was just one such person, or so he hoped. He continued, "I will be honest with you, I don't know much about the previous Vicar here, in fact I never met him."

Well at least he had not told any untruths yet, but he would have to do much better than this. Dirk coughed. Jack was uncomfortably aware that these moments of reflection for him were moments of silence for the listeners. He glanced at the organ, "Actually, I have a funny story to tell you, one of the first things that you hear in the church is the lovely old organ and I noticed that nobody's sitting in front of it, and you know old Dirk, I'm sure you do, well he's not that old, I guess you are as old as you feel, well old Dirk said that the regular organist has the flu. So I guess you can say that some folk are sick of me already!"

The silence was deafening. Well, however it was that he was going to win them over, if he actually did, it wouldn't be through his sense of humour. Although nobody laughed, Jack did notice that Mabel gave a smile and a gentle nod. Jack was struggling and then he caught sight of Dirk pointing to the numbers on the wall. He realised that they were hymn numbers, but what about the organ? Suddenly inspiration came to Jack, it was a gamble, but it might just work.

"Right, "said Jack, "I see about thirty people in this lovely church. Now given the law of averages, at least one of you must have some musical talent. So who can play a musical instrument? I would prefer the organ obviously."

There was a silence. After a few minutes or so, the lady in the early twenties raised her hand. Jack was relieved. "Lovely, "he said, "And what can you play? Please say it's the organ." The lady nodded and smiled. "Okay, why don't you come up the front and perhaps Dirk will wipe the seat for you."

The lady slowly made her way to the front. Jack was a tough and feisty fellow, but he also had a kind heart and could see that the lady was clearly nervous. He stepped down from the pulpit and walked up to the organ. As she arrived, he patted the organ and said "In your own time...actually I don't know your name."

The lady shook her head and looked down. Dirk coughed and shook his head. It then dawned on Jack that the lady was either unable to speak or was extremely shy.

"Well, whatever your name is, I am very glad that you're here this morning. You start playing, when you're ready." Jack walked back to the pulpit. The organ started to play almost immediately and he recognised the hymn, *All Things Bright and Beautiful*. The congregation started to sing and the young lady certainly played the organ very well. Jack was not religious and yet he felt much more at ease. He didn't plan to stay in this village very long, but at least he had met some nice folk. When the hymn finished, Jack turned to the young lady and said "Thank you that was lovely." The lady smiled in response.

Dirk walked up to Jack and handed him a Church Notices Sheet. Jack started to read it, then after Dirks cough, he realised that he should read it aloud. It covered a variety of items, the Bible Study Group, the upcoming Village Fête, the Youth Group and even a few Bands of Marriage. For the life of him though, he could not see where they would get their numbers from.

"Right," he said, "Let's have another hymn."

The young lady was still sitting dutifully at the organ. She began to play the second one, *The Lord's My Shepherd*. Jack was beginning to feel that the music and singing was making him feel more comfortable. He was also aware though that he did not really have a sermon to deliver. He opened the Bible. Maybe *Genesis* should be the subject. As the hymn ended, he thanked the young lady again. After he had thanked her again, Jack could not help but wonder if any of the congregation would be thanking him afterwards. He opened the Bible and read aloud the first part of *Genesis* and paused.

"You know, I've been thinking, what was the beginning like for you? Have you always been a believer? When did you first go to church? Did you go willingly? Were you dragged there?" Jack looked around the sea of faces. Well, if a comedian could feed off his audience, could a Vicar feed off his congregation? He got down from the pulpit and asked Mabel those very same questions. Clearly she seemed to like him, hopefully she would turn out to be a good sport too.

"Well, I have always believed, sir. I pray at least four times a day. I first went to church when I was baptised. I don't remember it though." There were a few laughs at her comments. Jack took a chance.

"I bet you would remember it, if I did it to you now, Mabel!" She burst out laughing and thankfully so did some of the others.

"Oh," she added, "I have always gone willingly. I also think that you are a lovely Vicar, even though I don't actually know your name." There were more chuckles.

"Well, Mabel, I guess some might call

me Reverend Parsons. My friends though call me Jack." He held out his hand. "Jack says hello to Mabel." She smiled, "Mabel says hello to Jack." Some folk actually seemed to be enjoying all this although Mrs. Thompson looked far from amused.

Jack stepped back "Right, who wants to go next?"

At first just one hand was raised and then shortly afterwards a few more. Jack walked around the church repeating the questions. Some folk gave brief answers, whilst others went into more detail. After he had talked to ten of the others, Jack returned to the front and said to the young lady still seated at the organ, "How about another hymn?" She smiled and started to play *Amazing Grace*. Jack was starting to feel confident. Whilst some folk had not smiled once during his service, there were definitely some who seemed to be really enjoying the experience. As the third song ended, Jack thought that maybe as it was his first service, some might expect it to be briefer than normal.

"Right," said Jack "My first service and nobody has walked out or thrown up, I'll quit while I am ahead. So, take care and God bless."

The congregation slowly got to its feet.

Dirk walked up to Jack and whispered, "You have to go outside and thank them for coming. That's always been our custom, sir."

Jack mumbled a word of gratitude and walked to the back of the church nodding to the remaining folk and then went outside. A slow trickle of people followed outside. Some thanked him and shook hands, although a few of them did neither. A nervous looking young man approached Jack, "Excuse me sir, I wonder if I might have a word with you?" Jack put him at ease, "Yes my son, how about now?" was the new Vicars response.

"Well, my name is Cory Jones. I have been married for four years and my marriage is fine, but you see, we don't have much money, so I am going to college and I am training to become a plumber. I haven't told my wife, in case I don't qualify, but I think she may be under the impression that I am seeing someone else. What should I do?" Jack could tell at once that this was the husband of the lady who had come to see him at the Vicarage.

Jack smiled," I will tell you exactly what to do my son, you tell her the truth, tell her what you are doing and why. Apologise for not telling her sooner, explain that you can't be certain that you'll qualify, but maybe she can help with your revision and so on." Cory grinned, "I say, I will do exactly what you said. Thanks Vicar, oh by the way, I loved the service. You are a real gentleman. Thank you so much sir!"

A few seconds later, he was gone. Jack could not help feeling a certain pleasure that at least one person, indeed two, if you counted his wife had benefited from his advice. Still he thought, it must not go to my head.

Mabel came up to him smiling "Thanks Jack that was fantastic."

Mrs. Thompson breezed past, "Come along Mabel, you must not monopolise this fellow," adding with a slight tone of menace, "Whoever he is." Mabel smiled "Don't worry, you'll be alright Jack," she giggled at her unintended joke.

Mrs. Thompson repeated Mabel's name and the summons was obeyed. Another couple approached Jack, They were an elderly couple. The man was in a tweed jacket and the lady wore a large hat. Jack could tell even at first glance that the lady was the more sympathetic of the two. The old man held out his hand, "Colonel Roberts," he said in an abrupt manner. His better half, well that was

Jacks guess, smiled and held out her hand.

"Abigail Roberts. A very interesting service, may I call you Jack?" The new Vicar knew that making friends was going to be essential here.

"Yes my dear, that is quite alright."

She smiled back, "Me and my husband are the Church Wardens here. We did not expect you to arrive so soon, but I can see that the congregation have definitely taken a shine to you. Wouldn't you agree Edward?" The colonel gave a non-committal grunt. Abigail continued, "You must come along and have afternoon tea with us one Sunday. I suppose that you are not married?" Jack had to be careful. Even though he did not wear a wedding ring, he did not want to tell too many untruths, but there again, if he did say that he was married, the folk would wonder where his wife was. He tried his best, "Well actually, I am married. My missus, I mean to say my good lady will probably come down in a few months...you know how it is." Abigail's nod told him that she did.

The next two that he saw were a middle aged lady and the young woman who had played the organ. The middle aged lady said, "Thank you so much for your kindness towards Sophie. She can be nervous at times. She has fantastic eyesight, very good hearing, but alas she does not have the gift of speech. I guess you could say that her musical skills are her way of communication with the outside world." Jack was a tough character, but he had always a soft spot for anyone who was unlucky in life. He held out his hand, "Well Sophie, I am so glad that you were able to help me out. Perhaps you could do this on a regular basis? You know, support your local Vicar. This evening would be great." Sophie beamed and nodded, gently shaking his hand. The other lady also shook his hand.

"My name is Stephanie, I am her aunt and I must say that you are a huge improvement on the other bloke, I mean Vicar." Jack grinned "Well ladies, you can't please everyone but you know the saying, its quality not quantity that counts and I am glad that you two are on my side." The two ladies smiled and walked slowly away. About two minutes later, Dirk tapped him on the shoulder "Well sir, you did very well." Jack knew that he had to keep this fellow on his side. "And so did you my son, so did you."

The journey back to the Vicarage was a bit of a blur. A few folk waved, Jack waved back and in the next to no time he was in the lounge although Dirk kept referring to it as the drawing room. Dirk mentioned that he would attend to the Sunday lunch and reminded Jack about the Evensong service.

"Six thirty sharp, sir," he said. Jack had not expected much for lunch and he was not disappointed. It was spaghetti on toast with three slices of bread and butter.

"That's not all sir," said Dirk. Jack had his expectations temporarily lifted and then almost as quickly sunk when Dirk brought in a cup of tea. Well, it was not as if he was the proper Vicar, although he reasoned Dirk did not know that, did?

Jack consumed his lunch and laid down on the sofa. He had earned his rest and surely even Vicars could be sprawled on the settee. Dirk came in and asked Jack if he would like to hear some music. Jack agreed, it was rather silent in this big old house. From another room in this grand house, he heard the music. A choir was singing. Previously, he would have yelled at his wife to turn it off or do it himself, but as the controls were out of reach, he guessed that he would have to endure it...for now. As one song followed another, he suddenly heard one that he really liked. It was stirring and yes he recognised it, *When The Saints Go Marching In*, he could remember the times when he would hear The Salvation Army playing that song in his local shopping precinct. He was so moved by this one that he moved himself off the sofa. He walked into the hallway and then followed where the sound was coming from. He went into the kitchen past Dirk and opened a door that he had previously not noticed.

This new room was huge with a settee, a couple of bookcases, coffee table and an old wind up gramophone. Dirk coughed, "More tea, sir?" Jack nodded. Well the tea was nothing special, but he had to admit that he had tasted far worse. Before Dirk vanished, Jack asked him, "That's lovely, do we sing this in our church?" Dirk shook his head. Jack would not be shaken off.

"Why not?" Dirk shrugged his shoulders. "Come on, why not?" Jack persisted. There was a significant silence. "Well sir, the villagers here are rather traditional. I guess some are a bit dour." Jack could not really argue with that, but there again for better or worse he was the acting Vicar and maybe it was time to brighten things up a bit.

As Dirk departed, it occurred to Jack that there might be some old hymn books and music sheets. He looked around and saw a wooden rack. He remembered that the name of these things. Yes, they were called Canterbury's. He looked amongst the papers. Yes, there were some music sheets. Well he thought to himself, this morning I met them, this evening they will meet me.

As Jack made his way back to the lounge, he noticed the various portraits of stern looking men on the wall. He had seen them previously but had not really taken them in. He noticed the famous dog collars. They were obviously the previous Vicars of this parish and not one of them looked either friendly or approachable.

"I guess you don't approve," he asked the portraits rhetorically. "Well I'll make the villagers smile, even if you won't." He stopped. He realised that he was being silly, talking to pictures and yet he felt a sense of destiny. Why did he end up here? Why was he wearing a Vicars costume when he was discovered in the boat? Why was he not thrown out of the boat? Finally, why was he, a chirpy cockney, the latest in a long line of stern and humourless looking Vicars? He was different. He wasn't like them at all and yet maybe that was precisely the reason for his presence. Maybe this village and its people needed a real outsider.

Dirk interrupted him, "Your tea sir." Jack thanked him

"Look, why don't you call me Jack?" Dirk looked shocked.

"I can't do that sir. You are the Vicar. No sir, I can't do that." Clearly this would require some work.

Jack returned to the lounge with his tea and noticing a newspaper, he started to thumb through it. An article caught his eye. It dealt with the issue of falling church attendance, it also mentioned that fewer folk wanted to become Vicars. No wonder that some folk were really pleased to see him. The nagging doubt was that he was not a Vicar. He had not been trained and his knowledge of the church was pretty much zero.

His main working life consisted of working as a removal man, a furniture dealer and for the last thirty years, the motor car trade. He had known some characters in his time, chancers, spivs, even a few bruisers, but that sort of lifestyle was not for him. Yet, here he was, pretending to be something he was not, giving advice that he was not qualified to give and living in a house that he had no legal right to. There was one course open to him. Try to do some good, be nice, be decent and then leave as soon as possible before the real Vicar showed up.

Chapter Four

As six o'clock approached, Jack had already resolved what to do for the Evensong service. He knew that he would either sink or swim, but at least there might be some folk in the congregation who might throw him a pair of water wings. Dirk was ready to take him on the trusty motorbike and Jack found that he was even looking forward to going. As they arrived the church door was already open and he could see about twenty folk in there already. Dirk commented that this was a good number for the time of day.

As Jack walked to the front, he saw the regulars, Mabel, Sophie, the Colonel and Mr. Roberts and alas the ever disapproving Mrs. Thompson. Jack spoke briefly to all of them and received the expected responses. He knew this could be a gamble, but as he would not be there much longer, he would take it and now was the time.

Jack looked up from his rough notes, there were now about forty folk in the church.

"Good evening folks. I was reading a newspaper in the Vicarage just a few hours ago and without boring you...too much."

There was a little laughter. That Mabel, she was really something else, Jack thought.

"It was about church attendance, it's falling my friends and the number of men and woman who want a career in the churches, well that's falling too. So I asked myself a question...why? Well, what do you think? Is it that some folk don't believe any more? Maybe some folk do believe, but they just can't be bothered to attend? Maybe, just maybe, some folk are genuinely curious about the church, but they don't think that they would be welcome. So, my friends I ask you, yes you as Christians, what would you do if you saw a new face in this church? Would you go up and speak to them? Would you say a word of welcome? This applies to both issues, why some folk don't attend and why some don't want a career in the church."

Jack looked around at the sea of faces. Some were sad and thoughtful. Both Mrs. Thompson and Colonel Roberts were cold and almost menacing. Jack noticed that a couple were muttering to each other.

"Can anybody remember the last time that a new face appeared in this church? Well apart from me. Can anybody amongst you?" The congregation clearly could not. A few people shook their heads. "Clearly we have got our work cut out for us, haven't we?" A few heads nodded. "We will return to this sometime in the future." Jack added.

Jack was pleased with his progress so far. He could tell that the congregation were starting to think. Maybe a few consciences were being pricked. Now he was ready to go to the next stage.

"You know folks, I think that we should never be frightened to do something bold and different, so we are going to sing a song that probably hasn't been sung here for quite a while, indeed perhaps never." Jack gestured to Sophie.

As she walked to the organ, Jack reached over and gave her one of the sheets. She looked surprised but still gave a smile. Jack walked around the church handing out copies to some of the congregation.

"I'm afraid folks that some of you will have to share, but still, it's a great way to make friends."

The music began and the congregation started to sing. At first they were very hesitant, but then they started to liven up. Jack could see Cory Jones singing heartily with April beside him. She gave Jack a wave. Obviously

they were on good terms again. Sophie seemed to be enjoying herself and Mabel was starting to move around as if she was almost dancing. As the song concluded, it was almost as if a barrier had broken down.
"Thanks Sophie," said Jack, "I think we woke a few people up just then." The song, *When The Saints Go Marching In*, had gone down very well.

As the congregation sat down, Jack could tell that apart from a few disapproving faces near the front, that the people had enjoyed it. He opened the Bible and started to read aloud a further two chapters from Genesis. Jack looked up from his Bible and said "I guess that a lot of folks are tempted in their lives and none of us are really perfect. My opinion is that we should try to do the best that we can, we should try to do good, and we should try to avoid doing wicked and sinful things." The congregation nodded. "I'll tell you what folks, why don't you go home tonight and read these passages again. The ones from this morning and the ones from this evening. See how it makes you feel. I would actually be interested to get some feedback here folks." Jack looked around and saw that Sophie was still seated at the organ.

"Right, let's have another song. How about number thirty-two, Sophie?"

She smiled. As the congregation began to sing, "Abide with me," Jack started to feel at ease in the church. Yes, it was pure coincidence that he was here. Wasn't it?

As the hymn finished, Jack noticed that a message had been placed in front of him. Dirk was always diligent.

"Right folks, just before you go, do remember that there is a Bible study on Tuesday evening and a Church Fête on Saturday afternoon. So, try and go to one of these or even two. You never know, you might enjoy yourself." The sea of smiling faces really felt reassuring to Jack.

"Oh, just one thing folks, "he added, "How about a round of applause for Sophie. The music has been great, perhaps one day, the singing will match it!" The congregation laughed and applauded. To be fair, both Mrs. Thompson and Colonel Roberts did applaud in a lukewarm manner, although neither appeared to be eager to laugh. Jack walked to the back of the church, nodding to the congregation and then went outside.

As the congregation filtered out, there were smiles, a few words of thanks and quite a few handshakes. An elderly and somewhat nervous lady shook hands.

"I don't supposed that I could have a word with you, Vicar?" she asked. Jack nodded and said that she certainly could. "Well, I live in a rather old house, and I don't know why this has happened, I am a clean living, Church going lady, but I think that there is a ghost in my house. In the last few months, the place is much colder and I keep hearing faint footsteps and even a few bumps. I've even heard a few cries. The previous Vicar used to scoff at such things, he reduced many people to tears, but I just know that something is not right. Please could you come and visit sir?" She started to sob, "Please help me, I can't sleep at night, I'm really scared."

Jack did not usually have much time for ghost stories and peoples accounts of the unusual and paranormal, but he could not help but feel sorry for this lady. He noticed that Dirk had walked up behind her. Dirks face gave nothing away.

"Look, I don't know what your name is sweetheart, but you seem to be having a really rough time, I'll tell you what, me and Dirk will pop around in a couple of hours, I can't promise that I can help, but I will give it my best shot." Dirk nodded and said, "We'll see you later, Mrs. Johnson. If we can help, we will." As the lady departed with a faint smile, Jack realised that this could be a very tough job, maybe even a very dangerous one. Whilst it was true that a lot of folk did not believe in those kinds of stories, they were still very frightened by the unknown.

As the rest of the congregation drifted out, Jack saw a smiling Mabel, a beaming Sophie and then Barney with a sad and forlorn look.

"What's the matter, Barney? Surely my sermon wasn't that bad?" Jack exclaimed. Barney shook his head. He was obviously very upset about something.

"Well, I've just been offered accommodation in another village. I will have my own bedroom, a shower, a kitchen and it's free of charge."

Jack was puzzled. Wasn't this good news? Before he could say this, Dirk jumped in, "So what's wrong with that Barney?"

Barney replied, "Well, they won't allow pets. I can't abandon Munchkin. He's the only real friend that I have. A lot of villagers don't like me. He is always at my side, he doesn't care that I have no money. Truth be told, I prefer dogs to most humans."

As Jack caught sight of an angry looking Mrs. Thompson, he could feel some sympathy for the last remark.

"Look, when do you have to move?" Jack enquired.

Barney replied, "End of the week, sir."
Jack took control, "Look Barney, me and Dirk will try to find a home for him, a nice home and... if we can't, we will keep him ourselves. How about that? The two nicest blokes in the village!"

Dirk flinched a bit, but Barney was overjoyed.

"Why sir, you are fantastic. You're the best Vicar that we ever had. Thank you sir, why, you are a gentleman!"

As he left, Dirk said "That's the first time that I have ever seen Barney so happy about something." Jack could not help but feel that he was really starting to feel at ease in his position. Could this last?

"Went well sir," said Dirk. "The villagers really like you." Jack felt good. He used to pretend to be arrogant to wind people up, but inwardly he wasn't as confident as he liked to make out. This praise from Dirk and other compliments too, were really making him feel both happy and appreciated. At that moment, Barney came back.

"Sir, I wonder if I might replay your kind deed."

Jack waved the gesture away, "That's alright my son, it is my duty to help." Barney though would not be put off.

"Sir, I could not help but notice that the church organ is a bit scratched, I might be able to spruce it up for you. Give it a nice shine." Jack had, had some experience of furniture restoration, but he could see that this man really needed to feel useful and capable, and anyway what was the worst that could happen?

"Okay," he conceded, "you can take the keys to the church and have a go." Barneys face lit up, "Why sir, it will be a pleasure." Dirk handed him a set of keys, and off, the soon to be ex-villager, went.

Chapter Five

Dirks journey back to the vicarage was just a blur to Jack, even though he was getting used to the speed. They arrived in next to no time, and Dirk offered to make some tea and crumpets. Jack was not a big fan of Dirks culinary skills, but he was hungry and pot luck seemed to be more attractive than nothing.

As Dirk went inside, Jack stayed outside in the front garden and gazed wistfully at the bright stars above. Although he had been an agnostic for most of his life, he could not help feeling that the beautiful lights in the sky and the beautiful planet that he and the others lived on were such wonderful sights to behold that surely all this could not have come about by mere chance or accident. Where there was art, there was also an artist.

Dirks cough made him jump. He stood in front of the doorway with a tray of tea, crumpets and what looked like strawberry jam.

"I hope that I did not make you jump sir, but your tea is ready and it is not a good idea to go exploring in the front garden in the dark."

Jack grinned and went inside. He walked into the kitchen closely followed by his ever loyal new friend and gestured for him to sit down.

Jack began," This business with Mrs. Johnson? What is she really like?" Dirk hesitated and then told him about the lady in question. Apparently, she had moved to the village about twenty years ago. She was, married at the time, but her husband was an austere and unfriendly man. He died a few years later. She was a very lonely, and consequently she was delighted when her sister moved in with her. Sadly her sister died the previous year. Mrs. Johnson was a very nice lady, but she was very shy and knew very few folk in the village. The church had brought her no actual friends. The previous Vicar was offhand with her. She was supposedly well off, but money had brought her neither happiness nor peace of mind.

Jack nodded his head, "Well, we might as well help her if we can." Dirk grinned and said," You might get some nicer tea and crumpets, sir."

Jack smiled. It was almost certainly true, Dirk was a decent bloke and he did not deserve a sharp or unkind response. Yes, Jack was really getting a conscience!

"I don't suppose that anything like this has happened before?" he asked.

Dirk shook his head.

"Well, sir I guess there is a first time for everything." Jack could only agree with that. It promised to be an unforgettable evening.

A sudden thought occurred to Jack, what could he actually do to help Mrs. Johnson? He wasn't an expert on the paranormal and he wasn't even a proper Vicar. When Dirk returned to collect the now empty tray, Jack asked him, "Well Dirk, if we are going to go and do a bit of ghost hunting, what do you think we need?"

Dirk smiled, "Well sir, you are the Vicar, I'm sure your knowledge is far greater than mine." Jack tried again, "Come on Dirk, you can do better than that my old son. There's more to being a Verger than serving tea and crumpets." Dirk gave way at last. "Well sir, I would pray and ask for help before I leave and I would surely take my Bible with me. A smaller one than the ones on the bookcase. Also, I would take someone with me." Jack nodded and grinned.

"Like a Verger, Dirk?" was his response.

Dirk nodded back.

As Dirk left, Jack started to feel nervous. This shouldn't be the case with him. He had been born and raised in the East End of London. He had had several fights growing up. He even had a few boxing matches when he was briefly in the army. Yet this was something that was completely outside his comfort zone. He was the sort of bloke who hardly ever asked for advice and certainly not for help. He realised that he was now pretty much on his own. Yes, Dirk seemed to be a decent and certainly loyal fellow, but how could he, Jack, take on some massive and powerful force that could quite probably be evil too? He looked around and saw a fairly small Bible on the table. Well, he thought to himself, it was worth a tray. Dirk certainly believed in it. As he stood alone in the room, he felt alone and vulnerable. He hadn't even noticed that the contents of the tray had been placed in a bowl in the sink but not washed. The Verger knew that his boss needed to be on his own.

Jack closed his eyes and started to pray, "Dear Lord, I really don't know why I'm here. I shouldn't really be. The folk here, they seem a decent bunch, I really need to be back home, they need a proper Vicar, they deserve a proper Vicar, but while I'm here, please help me through. If there is some sort of presence at this lady's place, please get rid of it. I can't, but you can. Please do it for her, not for me," he paused and the remembered, "Amen."

Jack felt a sense of relief. Could he have been wrong all these years? Maybe this was indeed real. Dirk was an unusual bloke to be sure, but he was no fool. Jack started to think hard and he found himself coming to the conclusion that maybe he had been wrong all these years.

"Please God, I really don't know what I'm doing," he called out and then again, "Amen," after another slight pause.

He looked at the clock. It was time to go. He gathered up the Bible and walked into the hallway. The ever dependable Dirk was ready, "Should be interesting, sir," he said, "The other Vicar never did anything like this," he added. The remark certainly hit home that time. Maybe Jack was here because he *was* different to the other Vicar. It still didn't seem right but at least he could see a few arguments in his situation. Dirk and Jack climbed onto the motorbike and began another journey. Dirk, the soft spoken country lad, was a real speed merchant on the country lanes. They finally reached their destination, a large detached house with a wishing well in the front garden. They walked up the driveway and Jack knocked on the front door.

After a couple of minutes, Mrs. Johnson opened the front door.

"Good evening, sir, I am so glad that you have come." Her slight smile that was coupled with nervous eyes confirmed Jacks feelings that she was telling the truth. She really did need his help. The only issue was if Jack could really help.

"Not at all, my dear. It's my duty to help, it's what I'm paid for." The words just flowed out, but Jack did feel a bit guilty, he wasn't a proper Vicar and even though he really wanted to help this lady, he still wasn't sure he could assist her. She led Jack and Dirk to the foot of the stairs. The carpet in the hallway was threadbare and there was no light.

"I'm afraid that the bulb went a few nights ago, and I am too frightened to go up and change it," she said. Jack groaned inwardly. Not only would be have to deal with a possible supernatural force, but he would have to do it in the dark! Jack was determined, he was not going to look for an excuse to go back home. That was a laugh, wasn't it? It wasn't his home at all. However, he would not baulk at grabbing any opportunities to make the task easier.

"I don't suppose you have a torch by any chance, love?" he asked.

"No, I'm afraid not, but I do have some candles," Mrs. Johnson replied. Before Jack could respond, she had gone. He could not help but notice that for an elderly and frail lady, she was very quick on her feet. She returned very quickly, maybe too quickly for Jack's liking, with a lit candle complete with a copper candelabra.

"Will this be okay, sir?" her anxious voice almost begging him to say yes. Jack grinned, "Yes, Mrs. Johnson that will be fine. Thank you." He looked at Dirk, "Okay my son, let's see what's been going on in this place."

Slowly but decisively, the two men climbed the stairs. Jack was used to power-cuts, but this was different. They reached the landing on the first floor. Dirk sneezed suddenly. "I apologise sir, it's my allergies." Well, it was a reason. Jack did not mention the fact that the noise had made him jump out of his skin. "Yes, you're probably allergic to the dark," he said. Suddenly they heard a noise, it sounded like steps, faint but quick. Then they heard a crashing sound and a cry.

"Oh my word," said Dirk, "This is horrible, sir." The steps continued. From his army days, where he had learnt many skills, Jack could tell that it was definitely a noise from above, but just what it was, he could not be sure. He saw some further steps directly in front of him, and he knew there and then that whoever or whatever was making the noise would be waiting for him and Dirk on the next floor.

Jack was tough, he had had many experiences in life, but he was well and truly intimidated. He closed his eyes, "Please Lord, help us, protect us, save us, Amen." It was not the prayer of an experienced and trained Vicar, but it was what he felt from his very heart. He felt some warmth for the very first time in this very cold house. He turned to Dirk. Whilst Jack had heard the maxim about safety in numbers, this was really down to him.

"You stay there my old son, I'll go it alone," he said. Dirk nodded, "Take care, sir. I will pray for you as you go up there."

Jack climbed the stairs slowly but surely. There was a tiny landing and then a door.

"Please God..."he prayed quietly. It would be frightening, it could prove fatal but he had to do it. He turned the handle and opened the door. He could see nothing at first, he held the candelabra in front of him, the light moving towards the middle of the room. Oh my word, he thought. Then he saw a pair of eyes, he heard a whine. He moved the candelabra up and down. There was a wooden chair that had fallen to the floor, or so Jack thought. He summoned up some morsel of courage, "This is Mrs. Johnson's house. If you are something evil, I say, be gone!" After a few seconds he felt something brush past his leg. This was worse than he thought. He also realised that he had left the Bible with Dirk.

Jack swung the candle light around behind him and there on the small landing was a small dark brown kitten. Jack swung the candelabra back into the attic room and then noticed the flames were flickering, it was then that he saw a window in the roof that was open. The pieces then quickly fell into place. Jack walked into the room and carefully using the candle light to avoid tripping over anything, he reached up to the window with one hand and closed it securely. He made his way back to the landing and picked up the kitten, which was surprisingly tame.

Looking upwards he smiled, "Thanks. No, I really mean it, thanks."

Jack and his passenger went down to the first floor and then below. The look on Dirks face said it all, "I just knew that you could do it sir. I was saying to Mrs. Johnson that you are a really special Vicar." Jack was a confident bloke, but this was a time for honesty, "I had some very special help," he said. Dirk frowned. Jack pointed upwards, "He came through for me. It could have been something very nasty, but it was just a non-paying lodger. Now tell me Dirk, who do you think in this village would like a nice new friend?"

At that moment Mrs. Johnson appeared, "I think that he has already found his home, sir. I have lived alone for far too long I think!"

Jack handed the kitten to her, "You're quite right, it is a male, you country girls don't miss much!" he laughed. However this lady was able to banter too, "Well, sir, as you are such a fine Vicar, I reckon that I shall have to name him after you, come along Jack, I will give you a nice saucer of milk, both Jacks if you like!" Dirk roared with laughter and after a few pleasantries they departed.

"Not a bad evenings work, sir," said Dirk. Jack could only agree. He looked up at the beautiful stars, "Amen," he said quietly.

Chapter Six

That Sunday night and Monday morning, Jack slept soundly. He did have a dream about the church. Various folk walking up to him saying, "Well done, Vicar." They were all friendly. At the end he saw Sophie holding up a piece of paper that read THANK YOU VICAR. He woke up. Yes, this had been a dream, but the feeling that he had was a very good one. For the first time in a long while he felt wanted, loved and most of all, needed.

Dirk brought him a tray with coffee, toast and butter. He informed Jack that there was a surprise downstairs. After consuming his breakfast and having a quick shower, Jack realised how true this was. Apparently the newest tenant had arrived, Munchkin. He had obviously been out for a run as there were footprints all over the hallway. He barked in recognition when he saw Jack. Dirk arrived with a mop, "No pain, no gain, Sir. But it is nice to have a pet around the house. The previous Vicar would never have had one," Jack smiled. Well he thought after yesterday evening, it would probably be a quiet day for him.

Jack and Dirk played in the garden with their new friend. Even a bogus Vicar could keep a dog amused. There was a loud bang at the door. Dirk said, "I'll get this sir."

This happened at least another four times. Finally Jacks curiously got the better of him and the next time that the door was banged, Jack pulled rank on Dirk. This was something that he did not relish, but this just seemed so unusual, "I'll get it this time, Dirk and that's an order, my old son." He ran through the house exceeding Munchkins previous record of dirty foot prints and flung open the front door.

It was the most unusual sight. A man and a woman with two large suitcases.

"Oh hello," said the man, "Are you the butler?" Jack was stunned. Admittedly he did not really look the part of a Vicar, but a butler?

"Actually, I am what could be called the new Vicar."

The woman smiled in response, "And about time too. We've got some stuff for the village fete." Jack remembered his manners and invited them in. The lady refused Jacks offer to take the case that she was carrying.

"You don't want to worry about her, sir. She is a farmer's wife, she's stronger than any man around here, apart from me of course!" The man chuckled. The couple introduced themselves as Mr. and Mrs. Perkins. Dirk appeared and it was clear that the couple were very good friends with him. Well that's another couple who seem to like me, Jack noted.

Jack escorted Mr. and Mrs. Perkins into the lounge, whilst Dirk disappeared into the kitchen. There was already ten other suitcases in there, all unopened. Mr. and Mrs. Perkins sat down and opened their two. In one was a lovely collection of dinner plates and cups. The other contained six well knitted cardigans. Jack thanked them and rejected the idea of making a pun about being used to giving services. Instead he asked Mrs. Perkins whether she had knitted the cardigans herself.

"Oh yes, Vicar," she replied, "I am pretty good in the kitchen too, I'll bring some food on Saturday, so it will be fresh. Mr. Perkins said, "We don't go to church very often, Vicar, it is very busy on the farm, but we like to help when we can." Jack was about to say that it was up to him but Dirk breezed in with the tea tray.

Jack was conscious that the crockery in his home was well below the standard of the items on the carpet, but there again they probably earned a lot more money that he did. That started Jack thinking. What would happen when the first wave of bills arrived? Who paid Dirks wages? Just a minute, there had been no collections on Sunday. He really had landed in the deep end, then almost as if he were addressing Jacks thoughts, Mr. Perkins pulled out a cheque from his pocket.

"Here you are sir, I guess that you could say this is our tithe. I guess a thousand pounds is okay for this month?" Jack could only mumble his thanks, mercifully, it was made out to St. Georges Church. Dirk pipped in, "I usually bank these sir...unless you want to do it?"

Jack was relieved. "No that's okay Dirk, I'm not here to upset the apple cart."

Dirk gathered up the cardigans and left the room without closing the door. Mr. Perkins asked Jack for his first impression of the Village. Jack was honest but cautious, yes some folk had been very friendly and yes, Dirk had been a big help. Yes, he was beginning to settle in and there was a new guest in the house. A split second later, Munchkin bounded into the lounge through the open door and knocked some of the cups over. To add to the impression, he galloped up to Mrs. Perkins and took a half-eaten biscuit out of her hand. Jack closed his eyes. He liked dogs, but this was very embarrassing.

"Munchkin, no. You must not do that. I will get some more biscuits for you love." The response was incredible from Mrs. Perkins, "Oh no, that's quite alright. I adore dogs. I would have saved it all for him, if I'd known that we were going to have company."

Mrs. Perkins started to talk about her previous dog, and how sad she and her husband had been when he had died recently. Mr. Perkins looked at Munchkin, "He's a big fellow. We could use him down the farm."

Jack realised that maybe, just maybe this dog could have a great and loving home. Yes, Jack liked dogs as did Dirk, but how long was he going to be here before it was discovered that he was not the new Vicar. And when they arrived, how would that individual react? Jack had yet to hear a good word about his predecessor here and the next one after Jack might possibly be worse.

"Look," he said, "He belongs to old Barney. Now he has found a new place to live, but they don't allow dogs. This is really a temporary home, but if you really like him, and you can give him a special and loving home, then you can take him with you. I must warn you though, he won't just leave his footprints in your heart!"

Mr. Perkins roared with laughter, "Don't worry about that Vicar, my wife is always telling me off for walking mud through the house. I have a hunch though, that *he* will get away with it." Mrs. Perkins was clearly thrilled, "That reminds me Tom you didn't get me a birthday present this year. He can be a belated one. Vicar, we would love to have him!"

Mr. Perkins grinned at Jack, "Well it's a damn sight cheaper than a bracelet." The couple left with their new pet and after they had driven off, Dirk said, "The place will seem quieter now sir, but the Perkins' are a lovely couple that dog will want for nothing. He will get his meals before Mr. Perkins and Mrs. Perkins will laugh about it!"

As the day progressed, there were more and more items accumulated at the Vicarage. Pots of plants, clothing, boxes of groceries and even packs of cigarettes. As the evening arrived, the ever dutiful Dirk reminded Jack that tomorrow evening was the Bible study. Jack started to read again in the lounge. He ploughed his way through Genesis, although he would have welcomed a teacher to guide him.

The next morning he decided to go for a walk through the village. The folk that he recognised nodded and spoke to him. A few folk that he did not know, still spoke. He had to concede that this was indeed a very friendly place. To top it all, he saw Mabel. They chatted about the weather, which was sunny but cool. He decided to take a risk.

"You know Mabel, the Bible is not always easy to teach. What would you do, if you were running a study group?"

Mabel paused, "Well, I think that the first four gospels in the New Testament are a really good starting point. After all, it is through Jesus, that we are all saved. Well, if we want to be!"

Jack realised now that if he started at the beginning of the Bible with the aim of going all the way through, it might be difficult for some folk to stay the full course. So, he would take Mabel's advice. Start with those books she suggested and then after a few weeks try some other books in the Bible. Mind you, would he still be there in a few weeks' time? Or even one? Yes, whatever time that he had left, he would try to keep the studies fresh and lively. He would chat to the folk. They could have discussions, although not arguments. It might even be fun! As Mabel departed, he received the heartening news that she would be there this evening. A friendly man that he did not know, called out to him on a bike. Yes, he did knew he had to leave this village, but he was really starting to feel at home here. Then came the nagging doubt. What would happen if and when, no it would most definitely be when, the new Vicar arrived? It was against the law, he believed to impersonate a Police Officer, but what about a Vicar?

Jack returned to the Vicarage and started to read again in the lounge. He found the first four books of the New Testament to be, not only easy to understand, but also very interesting. He looked at his watch and realised that he has been reading for a couple of hours. There was a tray next to him and the tea he sipped was cold. He obviously had not heard Dirk bring it in. Was Dirk extra quiet? Or maybe Jack was so enthralled with his reading, that he had been unaware of the outside world. He was now more sure than ever, that there *was* truth in what he was reading. He really *did* believe now. He closed his eyes and prayed, "I'm sorry that it's taken me so long, but I do believe in you. Please help me through this. I can't do what I should do, without you. Thank you Lord, Amen."

Dirk entered the room. He was a good bloke and Jack would try to show him that he was appreciated more in the future. Jack apologised for not drinking the tea and said that he was immersed in his reading.

"What part were you reading, sir?" he asked. When Jack told him, Dirk nodded his head and smiled, "Yes sir, my favourite books to be honest with you. I do like the Book of James too though." Jack made a mental note of that and twenty minutes later, the two were on Dirks bike heading for the church. This time, the village would have a Vicar that was a believer.

The numbers for the Bible study were reasonable. Jack reckoned that the final number was twenty-five. He decided to sit at ground level and make it an informal talk.

"Right folks. It's lovely to see you all, so let's jump right in. I want you to assume that a non-Christian friend or family member is talking to you about your beliefs. They don't share them. Now, folks, what would be your response?" Jack looked around. There was some shuffling and a number of eyes looked down at the ground. Finally a well-dressed middle aged lady put up her hand. Jack did not recall seeing her at church on Sunday, but then again, who was he to judge?

"Yes, my dear, I'm afraid that I don't know your name, but never mind that, what would be your answer?" The lady stood up, her voice was shaking. "I don't know, I wish that I did. I was hoping that you would tell me. My son has not been inside a church for ages. I wish that he did. I hardly ever see him, but when I do, he just ignores me. It's breaking my heart. You church people all think it's easy, but it's not. My son once even told me that he hated me for giving birth to him." She broke down in tears and then ran outside the building. Jack could see that this was a huge issue, but before he could question whether he could help, he resolved to follow the lady outside. He only paused to ask Dirk to take over the study group.

The lady was outside the church leaning against the wall with her face in her hands.

"I am sorry sir, I really am. I did not mean to ruin your class. I give you my word, I will never set foot in here again. Please forgive me for this."

Jack handed her a handkerchief.

"Look, you're having a really tough time dear. You don't have to apologise to me."

Jack knew that this lady desperately needed help. Could he actually help her? On the other hand, he might be the only person in the world who could. He just *had* to try.

"Look," he said, "Why don't you tell me your name and also tell me about your son. I *really* would like to know." Jack hoped that he sounded sincere.

"Well, I'm Gladys Carter. My husband walked out on me after two years of marriage and I had to raise my son on my own. I probably spoiled him and my late mother certainly used to. He was always a rebel. When he rarely went to church, I found out that my mother had bribed him to go. He always stayed out late, he drank, smoked and yes, he was on drugs, probably still is. One day, he came back after a three week disappearance, asked for money, I said no and he left. That was a year ago and he has never spoken to me since. I doubt though that you would even like him and you certainly would not want him in your church. The previous

Vicar said I was wasting my time on him and that I should just forget him, but I can't he is my boy!" The lady started crying again.

If there was a moment when Jack realised that he was really needed there, then this was it. "Where does he live?" he asked. The lady gave a faint smile through her tears.

"He does not live that far from me. It's in this village. One of my neighbours tells me that he lives with a lady. Apparently he does have a few visitors and they are not very nice looking men." The lady gave Jack a piece of paper with an address on it that was obviously handwritten.

"I so want to go and visit, but I just can't. I guess that you must think that I am pathetic, Vicar?" As she cried, Jack shook his head.

"No my dear, I reckon it has been an absolute nightmare for you. I will see what I can do, oh by the way, what is his name?" The lady briefly smiled, "It's Tony. Oh by the way, he has what you would describe as a Mohawk hairstyle and his hair is green." Jack nodded.

"Oh just one thing. Don't forget to pray, sweetheart."

Gladys refused Jacks suggestion to go back inside the church, but she did seem to feel better as a result of their talk.

Jack was suddenly aware of a person standing beside him. It was Barney, "Hello Sir. Just to let you know, I can clean the church organ after you've finished here tonight." Jack thanked him. It really was not that bad, but the last thing that he wanted to do was to hurt anyone's feelings and anyway, Barney could do with having a confidence boost.

"Oh by the way, Munchkin has a really good home now," said Jack. Barney smiled "Yes, I heard sir, thank you. Now don't you worry about that organ sir. Old Barney will make it look like new!" As he departed, Jack realised that the most important thing for now was to help Gladys and also her son. He would definitely go and see the boy, but then what? He knew that this would have to be handled carefully.

As the folk came out of the church, some speaking, others just nodding to him, Jack realised that whilst the village had been generally welcoming to him, there were certain elements that only socialised with each other. The word, clique, came to mind. He would definitely do his best for Gladys, but why hadn't anyone else tried to help her? Was she a lady without friends? Were some of the folk just indifferent to her? There really was more to this place than met the eye.

Dirk walked up to Jack, "I'm surprised at you sir, letting Old Barney clean the organ." Jacks puzzled look was clearly obvious. "Well sir, he is not the most careful of folk. He's no fool, but he is a bit careless...still you're the boss." Jack could see Dirks point. He was however much more concerned with Gladys. He asked Dirk to fill him in on the details about her. It seemed that she was a fairly regular visitor to church, but she always sat at the back or very close to it on her own. Jack could see that this would count against her in a closely knit village like this. The son was a bit of a tearaway and Gladys had been very lax in discipline. Jacks mind was racing. Could he really do anything with the lad? The immediate counter to it was, could he afford not to? Gladys obviously had nobody else to turn to and Jack also remembered that he was a rebel when he was younger. Maybe, just maybe, he could get through to the lad before it was too late.

Dirk and Jack travelled back to the vicarage together, and upon arrival Jack spent the rest of the night in the lounge reading the Book of James from the Bible. This was really relevant when it came to ideas about the church and indeed life itself. Maybe he should have been a Vicar all along. The one thought that continued to torpedo these bouts of optimism was the simple fact that he was basically living a lie. He was *not* the village Vicar and sooner or later the real one would most certainly appear. What then? His head was spinning. Should he stand up and confess to the congregation this coming Sunday? How would this congregation react? There were a few options open to him, but not one of them looked easy.

Chapter Seven

The next day was taken up with deliveries for the church fete. Whatever anyone thought about the villagers, and Jacks feelings were generally warm on this topic, there could be no denying that there was a lot of generosity. At least four rooms in the vicarage were crammed full of items. Dirk was even moved to say that this was more than they usually had.

"They obviously like you sir," he said, and on more than one occasion. Jacks mind though was more focused on the trip that he would make that evening. What sort of welcome would he get from Gladys son? Well, there was only one way to find out, he reasoned.

As the early evening arrived, Jack and Dirk set off for their destination. They found it down a long lane. It was a small, almost derelict, cottage with litter strewn outside. A rusty car and a couple of motorbikes were in the front garden. The dustbin had either fallen down or been kicked over. Jack looked at Dirk who could obviously read his mind now, for he grinned in response. The doorbell did not work, so Jack knocked on the door. There must be someone there, he reasoned, as there was pop music blaring out. He knocked harder and the music suddenly stopped. Yes, he thought, there was someone there alright.

After a few minutes a lady with spiky orange hair and a cigarette hanging out of her mouth, opened the door. Jack noticed that she was keeping the catch on it.

"Yeah, what do you want?" she asked.

"Hello," said Jack, "I was wondering if Tony was in. His mother is worried about him. She wonders if he is alright." The lady seemed un-fazed.

"What's it to you then? You're not his mum." Jack knew that he had to balance diplomacy with assertiveness.

"I only want a few minutes of his time. I'm the local Vicar, St. George's church. Lovely building. You must've seen it." Her response was somewhere between flattery and contempt

"You don't look like a Vicar," Jack steeled himself. "That's what they all say, but I am. Look, if you open the catch, you'll see Dirk you must know Dirk. He will vouch for me." The lady shook her head and closed the door. She hadn't slammed it, so maybe the trip would be worthwhile. To Jack's relief she opened the door. "He's busy," she said. Jack pointed to Dirk. The lady obviously did not know him but muttered, "I'll see." As she closed the door.

Jack grinned, "It's a good thing that we're not selling double glazing."

After about five minutes, the famous Tony appeared. He had green hair in a Mohawk style and wore a faded tee-shirt and equally faded jeans.

"Yeah, what do you want?" he asked. Jack was not going to be judgemental, after all that was hardly the Biblical way to behave, especially for a Vicar.

"Your mum, Gladys, asked me to see if you were okay. She hasn't heard from you for a while." It was hardly the most elegant statement, but it was the best that he could think of. Tony had a blank expression on his face, "I'm alright." His response told Jack that this conversation was going to be hard work.

"Look, if you just called round to see her or just phone her, it would mean a lot," Jack reasoned. Tony frowned, "Why?"

Jack looked at him, "Because she's your mother, she brought you into this world, took care of you and loves you." Tony shrugged his shoulders, "I'm busy," he replied. Jack didn't want to give up, but it was clear that the conversation was going nowhere. This was confirmed when Tony slammed the door.

Jack turned to Dirk, "Well, I know you can't win them all, but that was tough." Dirk grinned, "I thought you did very well, sir. The other Vicar wouldn't have even bothered to go. You tried sir. Don't feel bad." Jack appreciated Dirks loyalty but he couldn't shake the feeling that he should have done more. Perhaps he could try again in a few days' time.

"Just a minute," said Jack," Have you got a decent handkerchief, ideally an unused one?" Dirk nodded and produced it. Jack walked to the edge of the front garden and dropped it behind one of the motorbikes,

"What gives sir?" asked Dirk. Jack grinned. "Well, you can't leave your handkerchief here all week, can you? So, in a few days' time we can call back and say that you must have dropped it here." Dirk smiled, "Sir, you're unlike any Vicar I've ever met!"

As they walked back to Dirks motorbike, they saw flashing lights coming towards them. A car was being driven at great speed. "Quick," said Jack, "Get behind the bushes." Two burly men with shaven heads stepped out of the car. "Crumbs sir," whispered Dirk, "They don't look very nice people." Jack nodded," Well, my old son, I don't think that they are collecting for charity."

Jack paused, "I think that we better stay, we might learn something. Oh and it might be a good idea to say a prayer." The ever devout Dirk had already started.

The two men walked briskly up to the front door and one of them banged on it very hard.

"Come on Carter, we know you're in there," the man in the front yelled. There was no response, so the man banged hard again, "Come on, open up or we'll knock the door down." He turned to the other fellow, "Go round the back, he's not going to sneak away."

Jack then whispered to Dirk, "Stay here, but if the bloke gets in the door, move closer." With that Jack was gone. Having observed one of the men go around the side of the house, Jack quietly took the other direction. He felt that he must have drawn the short straw on this one as it was covered with brambles and stinging nettles, Remembering that he was technically a Vicar, he declined to swear, even under his breath, although his private thoughts were less sanitised.

Jack got within sight of the back door just in time to see one of the other men kick the door off its hinges. He could hear shouting outside and a lady's voice screaming. Jack leapt through what was now mostly the back doorway and saw both of the men punching Tony. Jack grabbed hold of the bloke who had come through the back and punched him clean in the jaw. He then followed up with a knee to the groin. The man fell down groaning. The other man left Tony and walking towards Jack, he opened his pocket and took out a knife.

Jack said," Put it away and fight like a real man." The bloke grinned and slowly shook his head. This was clearly going to be very dangerous. The lady, who was now clinging to Tony, pleaded with the fellow, "We don't have any cash, we're broke."

The man snarled at her and said it was her hard luck, but all the time he kept his angry eyes focused on Jack. The lady looked at Jack and sobbed, "I'm sorry Vicar, you shouldn't have come here." Jack now realised that short of a miracle, he would have to fight this very unpleasant and tough looking fellow.

"Well lady," Jack said," Just pray for me, no I'm serious." The man moved towards

Jack and then in a split second, a wooden guitar appeared behind the fellows head and smashed all over it. The bloke fell to the ground unconscious. Dirk stood there with a smirk on his face.

"Hope you didn't mind sir, but I have to earn my wages somehow." Jack thanked him and quietly gave a prayer of thanks too. He knew though, that he had to take charge.

"Right, is there any rope in this house?" The lady nodded. "Right," said Jack, "Lets tie these two naughty chaps up." The lady and Dirk got the rope and obeyed the Vicar.

After a few minutes the two intruders were tied up. Jack asked Tony if he was okay. The response, "Yeah," was enough for Jack to relax on that score. He gestured to Dirk to follow him outside.

"Right," whispered Jack, "This could be a small outfit or something much bigger. You must play along with me. Do what I say and don't hesitate. This lad could be in big trouble." Dirk grinned. Jack realised that this fellow was not only useful, he was rapidly becoming indispensable.

Jack walked briskly back inside and addressed the two captives.

"Right," he said, "You're not daft. You

know that this dog collar is just an act. I am *really* big in what I do and don't take kindly to any competition. Now, who are you working for?" Jack got out his wallet and pointed it to them.

"You better answer me lads, or my friend here will work you over. When he's not helping me, he loves gardening. Actually a pair of rusty rose clippers can be pretty good for extracting information."

The bloke that had fought Jack mentioned the name of his boss. Within a few short minutes he had also told Jack the address and phone number of the man concerned. Jack noted with approval that Dirk was jotting this down on a note pad.

Jack was now ready to bring things to a head.

"Right," he snarled, "How much does Carter owe your boss?" The yobbo who had received a guitar on his head replied, "Fifty quid," Jack opened the wallet. "Right, here's fifty pounds. Now I don't want to see either of you two losers again. Give this cash to your boss and don't ever come back. Tell him that there is a bigger and meaner bloke in charge. Oh and if you do come back, I will be ready, I will be nastier. And when I've done with you again, I will contact your boss and explain how I managed to get his phone number and address. There are others like me in other parts of the country."

The two men confirmed that they would not return to the village under any circumstances. Dirk untied them and they fled rapidly.

Both Tony and the lady looked at Jack with awe.

"Just who are you really?" asked the young woman.

"Well, if you went to St. Georges Church, you might find out. Your mum goes there Tony. Your mum wants to see you, you owe it to her." The young fellow grinned, "You're nothing like a Vicar, you're much more convincing as a thug." Dirk and the lady laughed.

"Well Tony," said Jack, "If you want to know which of the two that I am, where do you go to for the answer?" The lady smiled "To church." Jack nodded "Right. By the way, what's your name sweetheart?"

The lady grinned, "Shannon." Jack decided to risk a joke.

"Oh there's just one thing Tony. You better be there on Sunday. Remember, I know where you live and Dirk does have some rusty rose clippers!" Tony laughed, although it seemed rather nervously.

As they walked outside, Jack said to Dirk, "I noticed something in my pocket before I left. It wasn't your money, was it Dirk?" The ever loyal deputy grinned, "Oh no sir. Vicars have to have wages, even the unusual ones!" Jack roared with laughter.

Chapter Eight

The next day was a real blur. More items arriving, some in cardboard boxes, other items displayed in full view. Jack was wondering about other details such as food and entertainment, but he was informed by Dirk that there was a committee for that. Thankfully it comprised of folk that he got on with: Mabel, Abigail, and Stephanie. He did find out that Sophie could play various instruments, including the trumpet. The committee met in Jacks lounge and with the minimum amount of time and the complete lack of any type of argument, the event was planned out. After tea and crumpets, the ladies had taken all the merchandise away.

A short distance away, Mrs. Thompson and Colonel Roberts were also having afternoon tea, whilst the church was very much the topic of conversation, the Vicar was not receiving any compliments at all.

"I tell you, Colonel," said Mrs. Thompson, "There is something decidedly unusual about this so called Vicar of ours. There is no record of him at the Bishops office, and he doesn't behave like a proper preacher.

He really will have to go." The Colonel was walking a tightrope. Privately, he had no time for Jack and his unconventional preaching, but he was fully aware that his wife, Abigail, had a very positive view of this newcomer.

""Well Mrs. Thompson, if you have evidence that he is an imposter, then do feel free to confront him, for the good of the church and indeed the community," he replied, very carefully in his opinion.

Mrs. Thompson nodded, "Well, it just so happens that this Sunday evening, I have invited the Bishop to Evensong and then we shall see the back of this charlatan once and for all."

A few minutes later, Abigail arrived in the lounge, "Hello Mrs. Thompson, hello dear. I know I'm late, but we have been planning the fete. It looks like it's going to be really successful."

The Colonel nodded, "Yes dear, it is indeed very likely that the whole weekend could be an education for us all." Abigail not having been party to the previous conversation, could only shrug her shoulders. As for Mrs. Thompson, who rarely smiled, there was a cold but reassuring feeling of justice that would soon be served and that normality would soon resume.

As the evening approached in Kirby Maltings, one man who had a much higher opinion of the Vicar, was hoping to show his gratitude. Old Barney was not exactly an expert in furniture restoration, but he had been in the company of others who had done it. He opened his bag and got out some cloths, some gloves and the item that he hoped would make the church organ shine and sparkle in all its glory. He knew that he must not get fingerprints on the church organ, and so he carefully opened the tin, donned the gloves and poured out the mixture onto the cloths. The dark mahogany organ was about to be subjected to a most unusual experience. Sadly the music in the store had been too loud and Barney had brought and paid for a tin of paint stripper.

At the same time in the Vicarage, Dirk was washing up when Jack appeared in the kitchen.

"Hello sir," said Dirk, "Did you want some cocoa?" Jack shook his head.

"No thanks, but I bet that you could do with a hand with the washing up." Dirk was quite shocked, "Oh no sir, that is not a job for the Vicar." Jack decided to pull rank.

"Who is in charge here?" he said.

"You sir," said Dirk.

"Correct," said Jack, "So I am helping you with the dishes." Dirk grinned and accepted that he was beaten. Dirk mentioned in passing that when he had popped out to do some shopping that he had seen Barney. He was going to clean the church organ sometime that evening. He had promised Dirk that he would do a really professional job.

A short while later in the church, a clearly distraught Barney knew that this was anything but a professional job. They lovely dark mahogany colour of the church organ was now ruined and he had spilt some of the mixture onto the light green stool. All this brought back bad memories. The intolerant folk who had told him that he was useless. His so called friends who had borrowed money from him and never paid him back. His wife of just three months who had left him. Last but not least, the former Vicar who had always treated him with contempt. The saddest thing was that this new Vicar, this decent new bloke, had been let down by him. As he locked the church doors and looked around him, he hoped nobody would want to come in. He hoped that things would be better in the morning. He prayed, he begged that somehow things would turn out okay. He would have been pleased to have fallen asleep and to not wake up again.

The next morning, Barney awoke in the church. He had not slept in many of these buildings over the years, but he felt so guilty about the mess that he had made with the church organ. He prayed out loud that the disaster could be reversed. As he made his way to the organ and also the stool, his own eyes told him that his mistake was going to be discovered. He felt so low. He came to the belief that there was only one solution. Nobody really liked him, and nobody seemed to understand him. As for the few that *did* like him, well Munchkin was gone and this really decent new Vicar would probably never speak to him again. He realised that maybe he had wasted his life and therefore it was no longer worth living.

At that moment in the Vicarage, there were more boxes and bags arriving. Dirk was a man who had never thought he had wasted his life. This morning he was kept busy with the procession of goods. Jack asked him when it was likely to end. Dirk could only confirm that the fete was tomorrow. Jack did ask his friend if he would be expected to be there all the time. Dirk smiled and Jack knew that sometimes this could be ominous.

"Well sir, as you are our Vicar, it would be a rum thing if you left half way through the event." Jack realised that tomorrow would be a very long day.

As the afternoon arrived, and with it even more items, Jack realised that this was a really warm hearted village and this continued to gnaw at his feelings. These folks *deserved* a proper Vicar and yet he was really getting to like this role. It was true his knowledge of the Bible was very slim and yet he could see how the right person in the church could help and maybe even inspire a number of people. Like Barney, he was beginning to think that he had wasted his life, but now that he believed, he felt that his life could be turned around. The only uncertainty was how much longer this would go on for.

Chapter Nine

Saturday morning dawned in the delightful village of Kirby Maltings. There was a mixed feeling about the day. Some had been looking forward to the village fete, whilst others considered it to be a waste of time and space. Jack arose, had a quick shower and ate his breakfast. Dirk was cheerfully washing the dishes and dusting around the house.

Barney, meanwhile, was on top of the church roof contemplating what he thought would be his last day on earth. The villagers bustling around, unloading items and assembling stalls did not appear to notice him. Well, it suited him really. He was fairly sure that most of them did not like him and he felt exactly the same way.

Dirk's sidecar and motorbike arrived at the village green at a quarter to nine. Mabel greeted the two, passenger and driver, very warmly, "Hello Jack. Hello Dirk. It's a lovely day, isn't it?" said Mabel.

Dirk replied, "Yes, it is." Not to be outdone, Jack said "All the better for you being here, Mabel," and yes, he meant it. A few more Mabel's and the world would be a nicer place, a lot more like her and the world would be fantastic.

Mrs. Thompson brushed past, "Good morning, Vicar," she said with obvious disdain for Jacks title.

'I don't think I'm going to win her over," said Jack to Dirk. The verger smiled, "Well, you are one up on me sir. She never even speaks to me."

As the minutes continued more and more villagers appeared. Stephanie and Sophie came up to Jack. "I am so glad you are here, Vicar," said Stephanie. Sophie has brought her trumpet and she would love to play it, if that is okay?" Jack had only one answer, "Sophie, if you play it half as well as you play the organ, it will be fantastic. You go for it girl!"

Sophie beamed in response. Hearing her play gave Jack a sense of calm and relaxation. He really did feel at home in this village, and even if he had to leave and it was a sudden departure, he knew that he would never forget it. It was not his home, but it felt like it was.

Abigail Roberts arrived in her Range Rover, "Hello Vicar," she breezed, "I have never seen a turn out like this so early in the morning. You are becoming a bit of a crowd puller."

In many ways the mature lady was a bit like a teenager. Jack reasoned that her youthful demeanour was one of the explanations to why she looked and seemed so young for her age. He was about to offer her help unloading her car, when three other people stepped forward. Yes, this village certainly had community spirit!

Jack walked around the various stalls sampling jam, marmalade, cakes, biscuits and copious amounts of coffee and tea. His guess that some would be better than others was completely wrong, as every product that he sampled was superb. He heard a coughing sound behind him, it was Dirk his usual cheerful smile was missing and had been replaced by a grim and sad expression.

"You had better come inside the church sir, there is something that you really must see." Jack followed. He was unable to ask Dirk what the problem was as the verger was sprinting towards the church door. One man though did know exactly what the problem was. Barney now knew that it was only a matter of time before his new friend would find out exactly how Barney had let him down. Another five minutes, Barney decided and he would jump off the church roof and leave his sad and unhappy life behind him.

Dirk was already in the front of the church, next to the organ when Jack entered.

"Barney is a good chap sir, but this was too much for him. I am sure that he must feel really awful sir, in a much worse state than this organ." Dirk was torn between his loyalty to Jack and his sympathy for Barney. Jack was stunned at the sight of the organ with the French polish all lifted up. He remembered though what was written in the Bible, although unfortunately not word for word.

"Well Dirk, this certainly is not verbatim, but it says in the good book, that we should not judge." It was not the most elegant way of saying it and Jack was no scholar, but Dirks grin proved that it was appreciated and understood.

"You always seem to know the right thing to say sir," he responded.

A split second later, the brief moment of calm was interrupted by Stephanie racing into the church.

"Jack! We've got a huge problem. Barney is on the church roof and it looks like he is going to jump off." Jack knew he had to stay calm. He turned to Dirk and Stephanie,

"Right folks, I better get out there, you two do feel free to say a prayer, I mean it." He walked quickly out of the church. He knew that this was going to be very tricky. As he emerged outside he saw several folk standing together and looking up at a church roof. Jack prayed quietly, "Please Lord, help me, help Barney." Jack walked towards the church roof where Barney was. Before he could say anything, Barney called out, "Don't go near me sir. Let me die, I've let you down, just let me jump."

The crowd was stunned into silence.

"If it's about the organ, Barney, don't worry my old son. We need a new one anyway." Jack hoped that this sounded convincing. It was partially true. Barney was not having it though.

"No sir. I have nothing to live for, I want to die. I'm now going to jump." His last remark caused one lady in the crowd to scream. Dirk had caught up with Jack.

Jack whispered to his friend, "I need a ladder my son, really quickly." Dirk moved away. This was becoming a very dangerous stand off and Jack knew he had to play for time.

"Listen Barney, do you consider me to be your friend?"

Barney responded, "Yes sir, well no sir, not now." It was obvious that Barney was becoming confused.

"Well," said Jack, "Either I am, my son or I am not. It can't be both. I think of you as *my* friend though." Jack caught a glimpse of Dirk carrying the ladder. Thankfully it was an extending one. That was Dirk all over, even if you did not explain something fully, he just knew what you meant.

"Barney," called the Vicar, "I can't stop you from jumping off the roof, but as your friend and your Vicar, I think that I have the right to talk to you...agreed?"

There was a minute of tense silence before Barney yelled out, "Okay sir, but you are not going to stop me." Before Jack could climb the first step, Dirk tapped him on the shoulder, "Mr. Perkins, the farmer said that they have an organ that they don't use and this church can have it for free. He will even deliver it in time for the service tomorrow morning," Jack grinned, but Dirk had more, "That's not all sir, it is not that old and is much better than our one. Here's a photo of it with Munchkin." Jack thanked Dirk and took the photo with him. Slowly but surely he climbed the steps. He was too sensible to look down, but as he climbed this seemingly great height, he realised that this could literally be his last day on the planet as well as Barneys.

He prayed quietly as he continued to climb, "Please Lord, I really need your help. Don't let him jump." His devotion of duty was becoming so strong that he forgot to pray for his own safety too. Finally, he reached the top and was about ten feet away from Barney. He risked a joke, "Well at least you came to the fete." Barney started to sob.

"That's alright," said Jack, "My missus doesn't like my jokes either." Barney seemed defiant, "I have to do this sir. I have never done anything any good in my life. I let my family down, my friends down, even my dog." Jack tried to reassure him, "You have a new home Barney, I'm sure you will make new friends and get a fresh start."

This did not work, as Barney replied. "In this place sir, nobody speaks to me. I should not have gone there. This village isn't perfect, but its home. Do you know sir, I have not had a proper job for years. Anyway, I'm going to jump." The tears were running down his face. Jack silently prayed for help and wisdom. He knew that he would never forgive himself if Barney jumped.

After a few seconds, he knew that he had to say something, indeed *anything*.

"Look," Jack said, "I am not a proper Vicar, but since I have arrived here, quite by chance, I promise you, I have really grown to love this place. I would add most, though not all of the people to that. I now believe in things that I did not before. I have learnt things that I did not know before. I have been able to help folk, whose names I only recently learnt. I have not done this on my own, Barney, I had to ask the Lord for help. He has always come through for me, and I just know that he can and will come through for you."

Jack could see that although Barney was still crying, he was also listening and he appeared less tense.

"Now listen, about the organ; Mr Perkins, the farmer, is going to give us his to use instead. It looks to be in better nick than ours. So, how do I know? Well, Munchkin, his new dog is in this photograph sitting in front of it. The Perkins are both thrilled with their new dog. Now, I tell you what, you come down from here, and I give you my word, Barney, I will try to find you a new home and a new job. Agreed?"

Barney hesitated, "I don't deserve anything from you sir," he said. Jack climbed off the ladder and started to inch around the roof, when he heard a shout from below, "The ladders come down sir. Don't worry though, I rang the fire brigade a few minutes ago." The ever reliable Dirk was on top form again. Barney smiled for the first time, "I'm sorry sir. I keep bringing you bad luck." Jack grinned, "Its okay, I wasn't looking forward to climbing down on that thing." To Jack's delight, the fire engine arrived within five minutes and a very patient firefighter helped both Jack and Barney onto their ladder and back down to the ground. The crowd, which had gathered, applauded. Jack thanked the firefighter and somebody yelled out, "Speech!"

"Well," said Jack, "It may sound predictable coming from a Vicar, but I prayed when I went up there and my prayers were answered. Thanks to the fire brigade, and to Dirk and also thanks to Barney for giving the human race another chance, yes we can be pretty trying at times. Thanks also to the Lord." A number of voices said "Amen." Jack then added, "Now, I think it would be really great if we could help my friend Barney. Does anyone have an idea where he can find a home and a job?"

A tall man with a baseball cap on, stepped forward. "You know Vicar, I have been away from here for three months. I have a big house with a huge garden, and to be honest with you, me and my wife just don't have time to look after it. So, I will give him the chance to do a little gardening for us. Say three days a week. We have a log cabin at the foot of the garden, so, he can use that as his base." A few moments later other hands were raised offering Barney work, including Abigail Roberts. Jack suddenly thought that he might start crying. These folks were *so* nice. "You know," he said, "You folk are so fantastic. I am so proud to be your..." he hesitated.

"Vicar," said Dirk, completing the sentence. There was a huge round of applause, and cheering after that.

The man with the baseball cap explained that he owned a building firm and often went away on work. "My name is Steve Morgan. I don't go to church that often, but I tell you what, I will go tomorrow and support you." Jack thanked him for that and for helping Barney. Dirk explained that Mr.

Morgan was the wealthiest person in the village, and although he was a very shrewd businessman, he was a man of his word.

"He will do the right thing for Barney, sir, and that log cabin is quite big." A few seconds later, Mabel came up, "Oh Jack, we were so worried about you and Barney. It would have broken our hearts if anything bad had happened to you."

Jack grinned and said. "Don't worry Mabel, only the good die young, so I'll be around for ages yet!" Mabel laughed, "Oh Jack, you're a good man, but a bad boy." Her gentle slap reminded him of how his wife used to do this after he had told a risqué joke or teased her.

It occurred to him that his family and friends must be wondering what on earth had happened to him. He should have tried harder to phone, but he was hardly ever alone, had no mobile phone and quite frankly he had been quite busy since he had arrived in the village. His emotions were mixed. This was *not* his home, and yet he just knew that a lot of the folks here would miss him when he left. He prayed again silently for strength.

Chapter Ten

The next day, Sunday morning, was sunny with blue skies. Jack rose, showered and had his breakfast, reading the morning papers casually. Jack knew what he would talk about that morning, the Book of James. He jumped into Dirks sidecar and off they went. Dirk reassured him that the new organ would be waiting for them, and the old one disposed of.

"We get things sorted here," said Dirk. They arrived in the church grounds to see several folk going into the building, "The numbers are swelling," said Jack. Dirk grinned, "Word gets around when you have a great Vicar. They are probably aware of the new organ too."

Jack entered the church shaking hands and getting a smile of acknowledgement from everyone, except from Mrs. Thompson and Colonel Roberts. Well, he reasoned, you really can't win then all. Mind you, he thought, all the others more than cancelled those two out. Mr. and Mrs. Morgan were at the front with Mr. and Mrs. Perkins and the new organ, which was really beautiful and freshly polished, was there too. He thanked Mr. and

Mrs. Perkins for it and noticed that Dirk was looking at him and tapping his watch. Well if the Vicar was not genuine, at least the Verger was a professional!

Jack cleared his throat, "Good morning folks, I can't believe how many good people we have here today. Well, you are all welcome and we are going to start with a rousing song on our brand new organ, well it's new to us! The song is called, *When The Saints Go Marching In*. Our lovely friend, Sophie, is going to accompany us as only she knows how." Sophie moved to the organ and Jack suddenly noticed that there was a new stool too. As the singing and music started it gave Jack a great feeling of adrenaline and afterwards he smiled and thanked her.

"Right," he said, "Turn to the person next to you and wish them a good morning, please." The people responded positively to that, including those Jack had not seen in the church before. He felt that he was on a roll today.

"Now then," he said, "I wonder if someone would be prepared to come out to the front and read the Book of James. There's no pressure, but I want you all to feel that this is your church and that you are amongst friends." The ever dependable Mabel stood up and walked to the front. She read the whole book aloud and did so with expression and feeling in her voice. Jack watched the congregation. They certainly were listening. Some were nodding too. This was really connecting with them, he deduced.

Jack thanked Mabel.

"Right," he said, "You heard what Mabel said. We should not show any favouritism. We should not look down on other folk, and yet I wonder how many of us are guilty of such behaviour. If in a few years' time, the Prime Minister came to our church, would it be fair to say that a lot of folk would want to sit next to this powerful person? To talk to this individual? Even if they don't really like this person or voted for this politician? Would that make us hypocrites or perhaps we might say that we would be acting politely? As for a homeless person with no money, is it possible that this person would be ignored? My friends, we are *all* human beings and the Lord is ready to give his grace and mercy to everyone. I don't want to upset any of you, but we must try to like one another, whoever they are, wherever they come from." The church was silent. Jack felt that he had made his point clearly.

The church door opened. Jack was stunned, he thought that it was always left open during a service. It was Tony Carter and his friend Shannon. Jack grinned and he beckoned them forward. Although they looked different to all the other folk in the church, this really drove home his point.

"Yes, it is lovely to see new folk in this church," he said, and then noticing that Mrs. Carter was sitting next to a few vacant seats, he added, " Why don't you two fine people come and sit next to this charming lady here?" He pointed towards Mrs. Carter. As they made their way, the charming lady recognised her son and ran up and embraced him. She started to sob and said to Jack, "Thank you Jack, I mean Vicar. You've no idea what this means to me." As she hugged her son and shook hands with Shannon, Jack realised that this might be a bit too much for the three of them, so he said, "Right, isn't it lovely to see a family reunited. So let's give them a bit of privacy and have another song, Sophie, my dear, *What a Friend We Have in Jesus.*" As the congregation started to sing, Jack could sense a feeling of warmth and goodwill in the church.

After the song, Jack invited the members of the congregation to come up to the front and tell the church about any friends or family members that they would love to have joining them in church. Some mentioned their children, one lady mentioned her brother, one older member mentioned his cousin, but they had no car and lived too far away to walk to church. "Where does your cousin live?" asked Jack. When that person's address was mentioned, Shannon raised her hand and said that her car was back from the garage, therefore she and Tony could collect the person as they lived nearby. One young man in a suit said the one person that he would really like to see in church, was his boss.

"It's a question of real need," he said.

"In what way?" asked Jack,

"Well," the man replied, "He might become a nicer person and I really need a pay rise!" The congregation roared with laughter. Jack grinned, "Well my son, you never know just who will turn up."

The congregation went on for another five minutes with different folk mentioning different names, then sensing that this had run its course, Jack asked Sophie to play, *Onward Christian Soldiers* and after that stirring song he went through the various events and activities for the church in the next week. Jack asked Sophie then for one more song and after singing, *Put Your Hands in the Hand,* he wished them a blessed day and said that they would be welcome to return for evensong.

As they said their goodbyes outside the church, it was especially rewarding to see Mrs. Carter with her son and his lady friend. Shannon held out her hand, "Cheers Vicar, you're a real cool bloke, we won't come too often though, so don't worry, we'll just take that person to church and then split." Jack jumped in quickly, "My dear girl, Shannon isn't it? I would be worried if you two indeed three did not come more often. Sometimes my jokes need a bit of help!" Tony laughed, "Yeah, but you see, we're not married. You know as you church folk would say, we're living in sin." Jack replied instantly, "Well Tony or if you want to be precise, Anthony, the church can actually solve this sort of thing. You may need a few little extras, like a ring though." They all laughed and as the youngsters walked away, Mrs. Carter said, "I can't thank you enough. It's as if I have my life back. They're actually going back to mine for Sunday lunch. It's like

I have a family again." She left with a big smile and then sprinted back, "I've just had a thought, wouldn't it be great if you could be the Vicar who marries them!" With this last remark, she left.

Afterwards Jack realised that this was exactly the sort of thing that he would be dreading. Being asked to do something that he was not legally allowed to do. True he had done a number of things that he had never tried before or had even been trained to do, but *this?* If he did conduct the ceremony, the marriage would not be valid. No, he realised that he would have to leave and soon. Yes, some folk would be upset, but it was for their own good. He looked up at the sunny sky, "Lord please help me sort this out. I don't want to hurt anyone."

A few hours later, Mrs. Thompson and Colonel Roberts were talking in his massive library.

"You know, when the Bishop arrives and I have checked that he definitely *is* going to be here, we should be rid of this bogus fellow for good," Mrs. Thompson continued, " I could tell straight away that he was not a genuine Vicar, even if most of the village think that he is marvellous."

The Colonel replied, "I quite agree with you Mrs. Thompson, but my wife is one of those that share the majority view. We will have to be seen as reasonable." Mrs. Thompson took a deep breath. Whilst she was glad that the Colonel sympathised with her viewpoint, in her opinion, he listened far too readily to his wife's less traditional viewpoints.

She chose her next words carefully, "I have a lot of respect for Mrs. Roberts, but sometimes one has to be cruel to be kind. If, as I suspect, this man is an imposter, he has to be exposed and the sooner the better. I have made the effort to get the Bishop here and I really think that I have the moral right to have some support."

The Colonel nodded in response. He cleared his throat, "There is just one thing, what *exactly* have you said to the Bishop?"

"Well, I have told him that our, so called Vicar, has obviously very little knowledge of the scriptures and that he treats our church services like informal public meetings. He has also changed the style of the church, so that it is almost unrecognisable." The Colonel nodded at the various points, "Well Mrs. Thompson, I have heard that our

Bishop is a most learned man, so I feel that he will be able to detect a conman and a phoney."

In the Vicarage, Dirk was serving a late lunch of smoked salmon sandwiches and hot sweet tea. Jack was starting to wonder if this could be his last Sunday in this house. He just had this unusual feeling that something dramatic was going to happen.

"Are you okay sir?" asked Dirk. Jack thought to himself that this man must have some sort of sixth sense. Dirk just *knew* when things weren't right. Maybe Jack should try to bluff him.

"Don't worry about me, Dirk. We all daydream from time to time," he quickly added, "I better get my Bible, another meeting this evening!"

Dirk grinned, "A service you mean sir." Jack grinned back. Even when his Verger corrected him, there was an air of decency and warmth about it.

Chapter Eleven

As the evening arrived, Dirk and Jack travelled to the church. It was a dark and cold night and this amplified Jacks sense of foreboding. As they arrived at the church there seemed to be rather more than the usual number of folks there. Dirk had mentioned to him that the numbers had increased in the last few weeks that Jack had been there and yet...

There was a congregation of about a hundred people in the church. The usual faces were there, but there were some new ones too. Jack noticed a very smartly dressed man who was seated between Mrs. Thompson and Colonel Roberts. Mrs. Thompson looked at Jack sternly and then looked away. This new man, who appeared to be in his early forties, seemed to fix his gaze on Jack and was nodding as Mrs. Thompson was talking to him. Jack nodded his head to the new fellow, who nodded back but did not smile.

Still more folk arrived. The ever faithful Mabel came up to Jack and beamed, "Hello Jack, I guess you could say that you really *have* arrived. Just be yourself and you will be fine." Jack thanked her and as Dirk cleared his throat to signal that it was time to start, Jack made a final count at one hundred and twenty.

Jack decided that Mabel was probably right, "Right, Good evening folks, it's really lovely to see so many of you here this Evensong. I didn't know that I was that popular." There was a ripple of faint laughter. "Okay, we are going to start off with *Amazing Grace* and this will accompanied by the amazing Sophie." The smile from this charming young lady always made Jack feel that he was valued. As they song was sung, Jack started to feel more comfortable and as it ended, he noticed that some of the new folk were warming to the atmosphere and a few were actually smiling, although the new man sitting between Mrs. Thompson and the Colonel was not.

"Right, thanks Sophie, you are a really great musician, and we are very lucky to have you here with us." There was some applause. Jack picked up on that immediately.

"Yes, that's right, let's give her a round of applause and afterwards, why not shake hands with the person next to you and say, good evening." The crowd's response was even better than Jack had hoped for.

"Right," said Jack, "Let's read about the

Good Samaritan." Jack read the story aloud and then faced the congregation.

"Now, I am sure that some of you, perhaps many of you, would have responded in a similar way. *However*, how many of you could say that in the big world outside that you could name several folk who would have done so? If your answer is yes, you *do* know several folk just like that, well that is great! You mix with a lot of lovely folk. Yes really lovely folk. I'll tell you what, why not bring them to church and introduce them to this lovable and rather eccentric Vicar!" The congregation started to giggle. "On the other hand though, how many of you could say quite honestly that you could count on the fingers of just one hand, the number of folk you know that would have acted in the way that the Good Samaritan did?" Some of the people nodded when he said this, a few looked very sad. Jack did not want to depress them thought.

"Look folks, I know that the outside world is far from perfect, but when we go out there as Christians, then we are like ambassadors. If we do bad things, it makes our church look bad, but when we do good things, then it makes our church look good.

Just think about it."

Jack could see pensive looks on their varied faces. "Sometimes," he said, "We can help in sorts of ways. When I first came here, some of you probably did not think that I looked like a Vicar or acted the part. Agreed?" Mrs. Thompson scowled and muttered to the male newcomer seated next to her.

Jack continued, "However, some of you were just fantastic. My Verger, Dirk, he has always been my strongest and most loyal supporter and in a short space of time, perhaps the best friend that I ever had. Just a minute, we need to have some gender balance. My loyal friend, Mabel, she *always* has a smile and an encouraging word. I really appreciate it. Sometimes, no, I take that back, nearly all the time, I feel that I am not really good enough for you folk. You really deserve better, but the message that I take away from my experiences here is that I must try harder. I really do want to be worthy of you all. One day, I might even make it." Jack could feel his eyes were starting to well up. He noticed that a few of the others were dabbing their faces.

"I think that we better have another song. *It Is No Secret What God Can Do.*"

After the hymn, the congregation sat

down. Jack thanked Sophie.

"Right folks, in just over a month it will be Christmas Day. I am sure that I don't have to tell you the real meaning of this time of year, however, perhaps *you* could tell others. Why not invite them to our Christmas carol service? It will be candlelit, have lots of lovely music and there may even be some mince pies. That got your attention! If anybody wishes to volunteer to help out, they will be most welcome and appreciated." he looked at the sea of faces and apart from a few hostile looks, they seemed to be content.

After a further two songs; *All Creatures Great and Small* and *Everything Is Beautiful,* Jack thanked Sophie again and closed with The Lord's Prayer. He wished that he had been a Christian for much longer, but as he reasoned to himself, as he walked out of the church, it really was a case of better late than never. As he stood outside the church, a number of folk came up to him and thanked him for a lovely service. Mrs. Thompson, Colonel Roberts and the smartly dressed newcomer, walked out together.

They approached Jack and the new man spoke, "Excuse me sir, but I wonder if I could have your full name. I have reason to believe that you are not a proper Vicar and that you are here under false pretences." At least twenty other members of the congregation had emerged from the church and it was clear that they had heard what this new fellow had said, "Forgive me," he continued, "But I am the Bishop, so you can see that I do have the right to ask this question and I dare say it, a right to an honest and immediate answer!" The people that had gathered around were listening intently. So the moment that Jack had dreaded had arrived. He knew that the game was up. He closed his eyes briefly and in a moment of silent prayer, begged the Lord for guidance, wisdom and most of all, help.

"Well?" demanded Mrs. Thompson sternly.

"Alright," said Jack, "I'll tell you the truth. My name is Jack Parsons, I am a used car salesman. Until I arrived here, I had no time for religion and far less for those who practice it. Yeah, I suppose it is funny with a name like Parsons. Well, I visited a friend of mine one evening, we had a few drinks, put on some costumes, well his wife is into amateur dramatics and I chose this one, the Vicars. I took a taxi home, well I thought it was home. Well I ended up at the river, there was a great thunderstorm, a really powerful thunderstorm, I fell into a boat, it was in the river obviously and it must have been a miracle, not only did I not drown, but I ended up here."

Jack could see that people were stunned at what he had said so far, but yet there did not appear to be any sign of anger.

"Well, I guess that you folk thought that I was the new Vicar and I could not bring myself to disappoint you. Oh, I tried to slip away, but it did not work. I haven't even been able to phone my missus. Yet, I have learnt so much since I have been here. Some of you, well most of you have been so friendly and encouraging that even if I had got an opportunity to leave, it would have been difficult for me to leave." Some of the folk were misty eyed, some were crying.

"However, I *have* changed, I was not a believer when I came here, but I most certainly am one now. I prayed often and the Lord has helped me through. I prayed silently before I told you all this."

Mrs. Thompson was unmoved, "It is still a deception, Parsons, and you should be prosecuted." Colonel Roberts was slightly, but only slightly more mild. "It's not on, you know old chap. It is deceit, and I shall expect to see the books from the time that you were here. Well, you were dishonest about your job title."

Mrs. Thompson moved in for the kill, "When this comes to trial, I will be quite happy to give evidence against this charlatan. I sincerely hope that he gets sent down for a long time."

The brief silence was broken by a previous unknown voice. "No, no, he is a good man." The voice belonged to Sophie. For the first time in her life she had found the gift of speech. The stunned sound that followed was broken by Stephanie, who hugged her niece and said, "Darling, I always knew that you would speak one day. No other Vicar has ever showed you any consideration. I promise you dear, I will go to court and speak up for our friend." She turned directly to face the Bishop.

"My niece has been mute for all her life. She always had the gift of music, but never of speech. This new Vicar is the best one that we have ever had. He has made her feel as if she is valued, liked and even cherished. I know that he has been good to many others here as well."

Mabel moved forward, "You won't be alone dear. I am what you would call a regular church goer and I can say that he is a fantastic man. If there is a better Vicar, I have yet to meet that person!" A few seconds later, Abigail Roberts said, "I don't like to go against my husband, but I will also be pleased to speak in court on behalf of this truly wonderful man!"

She paused, "Personally, I really wish that he would stay here, would you all agree with that?" The crowd broke out into almost unanimous applause.

Steve Morgan handed Jack a card, "My younger brother is a really fantastic barrister so, give him a call. Say you are a friend of mine and he will win the case for you!"

Jack managed a half smile, "It's very kind of you, my son, but I can't afford a bloke of that calibre." Steve Morgan was unmoved. "Did I say anything about paying? I paid for his training. He would love to repay me for the favour!"

Mrs. Thompson glared at the villagers and turned to Colonel Roberts, "Well, I hope that you at least are not going to weaken?" The Colonel paused for a second, "Look, I don't approve of any type of deception, but dammit the folks *do* like this fellow, and look what happened to Sophie!" Mrs. Thompson refused to budge, "I never really did think you were much of a Christian, Colonel."

The man had often bitten his tongue with this lady, but finally he had had enough, "Really now, Mrs. Thompson, you must write down one day all the good deeds that you have done for people, I doubt that you will need a very large piece of paper." He turned to his wife, "Well, you should be happy my dear, you are not disagreeing with your husband anymore."

Whilst the villagers were celebrating the fact that they had stood up for their much loved Vicar and giving the Bishop their powerful and emotional arguments, one man was no longer there. Jack had decided to walk back to the vicarage. He did not like the idea of accepting charity but he knew this barrister would probably be essential. He walked into the house, collected a few items and wrote a brief note to his now possibly former friend, Dirk. It read:

Dear Dirk, I cannot apologise enough to you and the villagers. Thank you so much for your friendship and kindness in my brief stay here, indeed I have learnt so much, some of it from you. Although none of you will probably ever see me again, I will always remember this lovely village. I did gain something very precious, I found true faith and became a genuine Christian.

Yours Jack.

Twenty minutes later, he was walking along a long winding country lane. His luck was clearly not in, as it started to rain. This coupled with the dark evening would make some folk feel vulnerable, but Jack was just focused on one thing, getting home as soon as possible. He could hear a car behind him, he thought briefly of hitch hiking, but he had so far to travel that it would probably be a waste of time. The car behind him though seemed to have stopped. Jack grimaced, maybe they wanted directions to Kirby Maltings? Maybe it was the new Vicar? Mind you, that would be rather unfortunate as the car was travelling away from the village. Still, if they needed directions, as a true Christian, Jack would oblige, even if it *was* his successor.

The car's horn started pipping. Jack thought it best to ignore it. It pipped again. A vaguely familiar voice called out, "I say, Mr Parsons, you never told me where you live?"

It was the Bishop. Jack turned around in disbelief. The Bishop waved Jack towards the car, "I might be travelling along the same route as you." He seemed to be genuine.

"I doubt it," said Jack mentioning his home town quickly.

The Bishop smiled again, "It's on the route as far as I'm concerned, unless you enjoy walking in the rain, why not jump in?" The chauffeur stepped outside the car and opened the back door. Jack was still not sure, "It's very kind of you mate, but do you think it's a good idea? We could be facing each other in court soon." The Bishop laughed, "I don't think it's going to come to that Mr. Parsons, or should I say Jack. You left rather too early. The villagers were full of praise for you. Only one person and I am sure you can guess the identity, is against you. I would say that virtually every other person in the village would testify on your behalf!" The Bishop waved Jack into the car, Jack obliged. As the chauffeur closed the door, the Bishop said, "Right, I wonder if I could discuss religion with you? You may not have had any training, but you seem to have quite a talent, even a calling for it." The car drove off into the dark and rainy evening.

Epilogue

Just over one year had passed since these events in the lovely village called Kirby Maltings. No new Vicar had arrived and the congregation had had to rely on themselves for preaching and organising things. Even Dirk had been pressed into service more. They had prayed for a new Vicar for a very long time now and whilst some had given up hope, others believed that one would arrive some day.

It was dark on this Sunday evening, yet many folk still made their way to their church. As the congregation assembled inside the church, Dirk welcomed them and he also reminded them of the Christmas carol service next week. Dirk said he hoped that this would whet the appetite of the villagers for next week. He said in a proud voice, "My friends, I know that you are all as proud of this young lady as I am, please welcome Sophie!" There was a powerful round of applause as this gifted young lady made her way to the front. Everybody in attendance was willing her on.

As she began to sing, there were a number of moist eyes in the congregation. The ever dependable Mabel accompanied her on the piano. Reassuring though this was, Sophie as the only singer needed all the confidence she could receive. As the song continued everyone was genuinely appreciative of her smooth and most delightful voice. A person at the back of the church may have been able to hear the church door open and close quietly. As she concluded the song there was a huge round of applause. Sophie was not smiling though, and her eyes were filled with tears. It just did not seem possible, and yet it was.

Jack Parsons stood in front of her, in a Vicars costume. She ran towards him and hugged her favourite ever Vicar.

"Jack, Jack, I knew you would come back to us," she sobbed. The folk burst into more applause and many rushed forward to share a hug with *their* Vicar too. Jack shook hands with Dirk and put his finger to his lips, "Hello folks I hear that you are looking for a new Vicar and if you'll have me, I'll come back." He turned to Sophie, and added, "For good this time!" Mabel gave him a big hug and said, "I just knew that you would come back here, Jack. You just try getting away from us!" The congregation applauded again. Jack turned to Dirk, "By the way, there is just one thing. This time, I am qualified!"

Anybody walking outside St Georges Church would have wondered what all the noise was about, but to those inside, there was no doubt at all. Their prayers had been answered. A man who for several years had never heard of their village had now returned to the place he considered home.

Dear Reader
If you have enjoyed reading this book, then please leave a review on Amazon.
Thank you.

43483368R00074

Printed in Poland
by Amazon Fulfillment
Poland Sp. z o.o., Wrocław